CURSED SPIRIT

CURSED SPIRIT

AMY RAVENEL

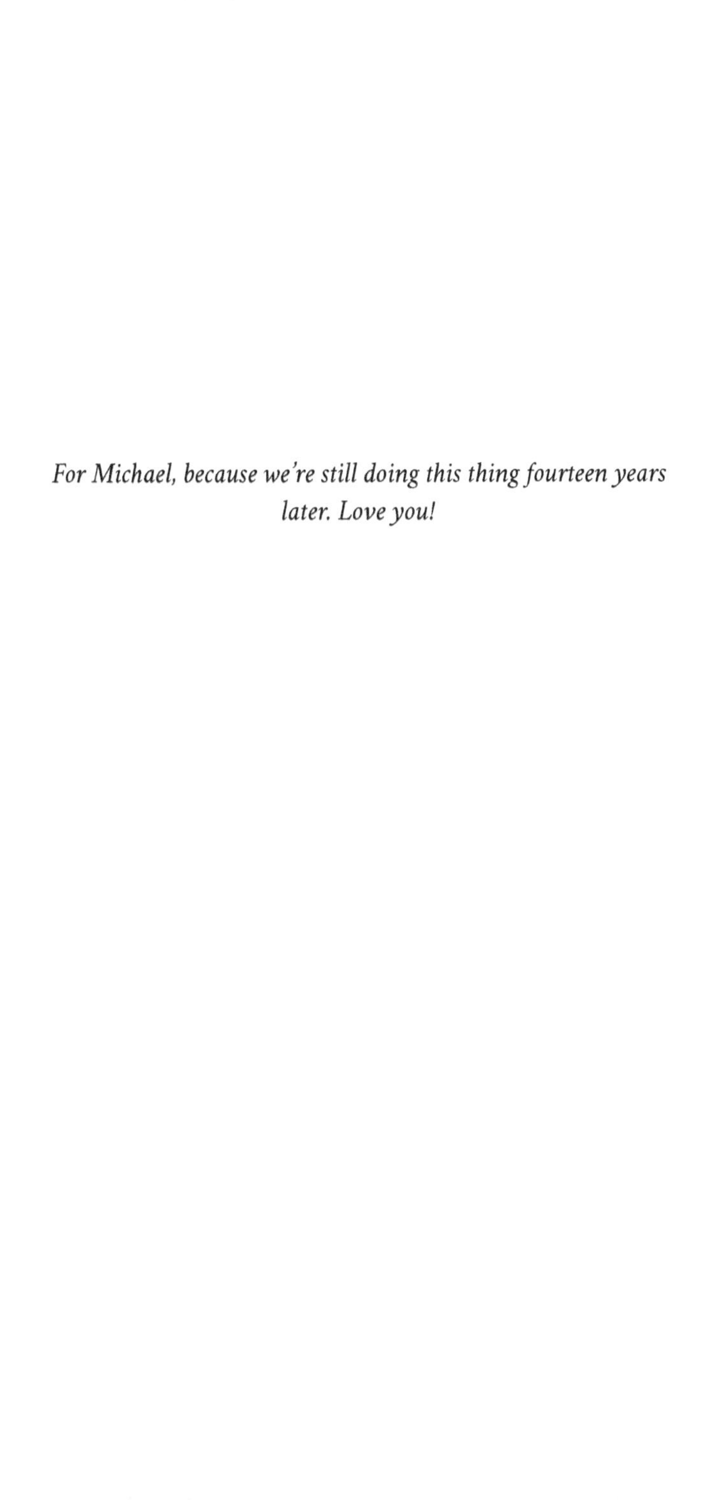

For Michael, because we're still doing this thing fourteen years later. Love you!

Ghosts wanted to destroy Drew Keane. He didn't have any proof, but he knew they did. It didn't matter what investigation he worked or how many people filled the room; the ghosts zeroed in on him.

One time, a lamp sailed through the air and crashed into his leg. The small scar still decorated his left calf. Another time, the ghost of a little boy screeched in his ear. His eardrum rang for days after. On the last job, a mean, dead woman pelted him with pottery. They cracked as each one hit the wall. The cuts from the sharp shards continued to heal, pink and tender.

During the investigation before that, the ghost of a dog somehow latched its teeth onto his leg. They didn't break the skin, thank goodness, but they ripped the back of his favorite pair of jeans and not in a cool way.

The White Lady of Hidden Forest Apartments from two months before was the worst of all. He remembered the brutal confrontation. Not only had she killed one of his best friends and sucked energy out of his other best friend, but her rage and unnatural strength put Drew in the hospital.

No more! Drew had had enough. Carrying around a clunky bag of salt and tossing the white substance into the air to ward off wayward spirits wasn't cutting it anymore. He plotted a plan and gathered materials, tools, and some free time. It was time to create the ghost disruptor he had been thinking about for a while.

Why hadn't anyone made one yet? He hadn't come across one in his research. All sorts of machines that claimed to detect ghosts flooded the market, but none of them repelled them. He wanted to change that.

Pounding drums and screaming guitars assaulted his ears, but Drew didn't mind one bit. In fact, Slipknot was his go-to band for concentration. Most people needed quiet while they worked, but quiet distracted him. Metal kept him right on task. And that's where his head needed to be at that moment.

He gripped the handle of a small Phillips head screwdriver and twisted a tiny screw into place. Bit by bit, his new machine took shape—a machine meant to break a ghost apart before he or she ever reached him. It required plenty of time to research electromagnetic pulse generators and adapt the parts he had, but the plans he drew came to fruition.

His boss Aaron Lawson groaned when he mentioned the idea. He worried that this new tech would mess with the rest of the computers and gadgets they used. To be fair, his fears were not unfounded, but Drew continued to work and tweak. He reached for another screw, careful not to drop it and lose it under the bulkier mechanical equipment that filled his supply closet-sized office.

The metal increased in intensity and so did Drew's work. His jaw ached from clenching it for so long. Just a couple more screws. That's all he needed.

Slipknot cut off the moment his cell phone spit out his Black Sabbath ringtone. He glanced over, ready to ignore it when he saw "Mom" displayed on the screen. She'd never forgive him if he didn't answer.

"Hey, Mom!"

"Drew! I hope I'm not bothering you." His mother's light voice came through cheerful and clear.

Drew lifted his head and rubbed his weary eyes. "You never bother me, Mom. What's going on?"

"Well, I wanted to find out your plans for Thanksgiving before Greg whisks me away on our cruise." He pictured his mother tossing her head back in a laugh, her frosted, short hair bouncing in a breeze. Her blue eyes shined like she had a secret to tell.

"I'm coming to your house like I always do. Wouldn't miss your turkey for the world." Drew stretched and popped his back. How long had he been sitting in his chair? One look at the clock on his desktop told him it was late afternoon, and he had missed lunch. Again. Why hadn't anyone come to check on him?

His mother cleared her throat. "Well, I thought, maybe, you'd might like to reconnect with your dad."

Drew's good mood plummeted. "Why would I want to do that?"

"Don't shut down on me. He came by the other night, and we had a good talk. He's been sober for almost three months now. He wants to see you."

Drew tightened his grip on the screw driver. "He's had plenty of opportunities."

"Drew."

"Mom." He barked out the word before he caught himself. He fought to control his breathing. Taking his anger out on his mother didn't solve anything. It only made her sad. "You tried to call him when I was in the hospital. He didn't want to be found."

"But I think he wants to try now."

He growled low in his throat. How could she still believe in his dad after everything he'd done?

"You didn't give him my number, did you?"

"No. I won't give it to him unless you say it's okay."

Drew jumped to his feet, dropping the screwdriver. It clattered to the old hardwood floor. He needed to move, to breathe. All of sudden, the tiny room shrunk, and the walls closed in on him. "It's not okay." His voice was sharper than it needed to be.

"All right. All right. I won't push. But I hope someday you can forgive him." The lightness disappeared from her voice.

Guilt gnawed at Drew. He hated disappointing his mother, but he refused to give an inch when it came to his father. He formed a fist, ready to punch something, anything. "I'm surprised you can."

He remembered how loud his father yelled, how hard he threw things. Darren Keane had a mean temper when he drank too much. He never hit Drew or his older sister Lori, but he almost smacked Drew in the head with a plate once. The yelling and throwing never lasted for long because his father passed out soon after. But when he wasn't drunk, he ignored his only son.

No, Drew possessed no forgiveness nor love for the man.

His mother sighed. "Your father wasn't always like that."

"I never saw him any other way." Drew took a deep breath. He didn't want this entire conversation to be about a man he intended never to have a relationship with. "Are you excited about your trip?" Distracting his mother was his best bet. It also gave him a chance to calm down.

"Oh, yes. I have a new bathing suit and a large supply of mystery books to take with me." His mother chatted about her upcoming trip for the next few minutes while Drew let her go on. He was happier when his mother was happy. One thing he knew for sure, Greg, his stepfather, made her jubilant.

After a few more minutes, Drew ended the call and promised his mother he'd be home for Thanksgiving. He took a moment to relax. One by one, his fingers uncurled from the fists they'd made. The intense urge to punch dissipated. Drew hated that his father angered him so quickly, even after all those years.

When he felt more like himself, he stepped out of his office and into the bright open floor of the Restless Spirits main office. He blinked several times, his eyes adjusting to the brightness of the sun streaming in through the large front window. Another item on the to-do list: buy a brighter lamp for his tiny office.

McKenna Ellison, resident researcher, client wrangler, and empath, waved to him from her desk. She held the business phone at her ear as she chatted. She was probably scheduling a prospective client for a ghost-hunting consultation.

That's what they did at Restless Spirits, literally bust ghosts. Or at least, send them on their merry way to the other side after proving they existed.

He waved back to McKenna and stepped out into the crisp November afternoon. At least it was sunny and bright, no clouds in the sky. He planned to enjoy the last few good days before winter set in and started dumping snow everywhere. It always happened sometime before Thanksgiving.

Popping his earbuds into his ears, Drew bounced up the sidewalk in search of a late lunch. Now that he was aware of it, his stomach rumbled. He adjusted his favorite Duke cap on his head and stuffed his hands in the pockets of his coat. He let his feet do the walking.

He didn't get far when he turned his head and saw a

familiar smile in the window of Mountain Peak Antiques. He paused the music as his heart stuttered.

Jaime Liu tossed her long, black hair over her shoulder as she laughed at something the woman next to her said. Her whole face brightened, including her light brown eyes. She was the most beautiful woman he had ever seen in his life.

He imagined the sound of her laugh, hearty and musical. Every part of him warmed, knocking out the cold.

With a grin on his face, he slipped into the large antique shop and ducked behind a rack of clothing. Peeking out, he made sure Jaime couldn't see him. He then bounced over to her and covered her eyes with his hands.

"Guess who?"

***

Jaime yelped and yanked the big hands away. She whirled, ready to punch the offender in the stomach. No one sneaked up on her without her knowing about it. Her fright melted away when she saw who stood behind her. Instead of punching, she threw her arms around him. "Drew!"

"The one and only." He lifted her off the ground.

She tossed her head back and laughed again. After dating him for two months, Jaime's stomach still did a somersault when she saw him. She adored his shrewd hazel eyes, his freckled light skin, and his mop of blondish-brown hair. She even liked the ridiculous Duke Blue Devils baseball cap he insisted on wearing.

Her friend Layne Williams cleared her throat as Jaime's feet touched the ground. "Did I walk into a fragrance commercial or something?" Her dark brown eyes looked from Jaime to Drew.

Jaime took a minute to catch her breath. "No. This is Drew. The guy I told you about."

"Wait. This is the guy who drove around aimlessly on your first date?" The stern expression disappeared from Layne's dark brown face.

Drew dropped his hands into his coat pockets. "It wasn't aimless. I knew what I was doing." He lied. He picked her up with no plan for that first date, but Jaime had seemed charmed anyway.

"Sure you did." Layne lifted a perfectly sculpted brow.

Jaime rolled her eyes. "So, you're antiquing, too?" she asked Drew.

"Oh, um, is that where we are?" He glanced around in wonder as if he hadn't noticed he stood in a large antique shop.

"Yeah, we've been here for a while."

He flashed that amazing grin, a teasing gleam in his eyes. "Actually, I was on my way to lunch and saw you in here. Thought I'd surprise you."

"I didn't know we'd reached the surprise level yet."

"I think several dates count as the surprise level." Drew took a step back. "But you're here with your friend, and I don't want to butt in. I'll call you, though." He took another step toward the door.

Though she had arranged her Friday afternoon to visit antique shops with Layne, she liked that Drew popped in unannounced. She loved spending extra time with him. "No, stay. Maybe you can help me pick something to hang over my couch?"

Layne patted Jaime on the back, but her eyebrow continued to stay its upright position. "I'll be over by the furniture if you need me." She glared at Drew, pointed at her eyes with two fingers, and pointed them at him before moving away.

Jaime waved in her friend's direction. "Don't mind Layne. She's a little overprotective."

"She's a little intimidating," Drew admitted. He watched her until she was out of sight.

"You're not playing hooky from work, are you?" She put on her best teacher voice, the one that made the college freshman she taught quake in their boots.

Drew shrugged, the grin never leaving his face. "I have a reasonable boss, and I missed lunch." He wasn't cowed. She made a mental note to work on her intimidation skills.

"Excellent." She tossed her hair over her shoulder, trying to look nonchalant.

"You're happy I haven't eaten anything yet?" Drew rested his hand on his stomach. "You want me to starve?"

Jaime ducked around Drew. "No, but I am glad you're here. I guess we can count this as our next date?" She walked around a broken-down jukebox. It missed a few buttons, and she didn't recognize several of the song titles.

He fell into step beside her and draped an arm around her shoulders. "A spontaneous date. I like it."

Jaime hadn't intended to date at all. Before Drew, she hadn't been on a date in more than a year. Not since that lawyer decided he didn't want a kid hanging around. But when she met Drew at the grave for The White Lady, she felt a spark. Her daughter Ella's withering stare didn't chase him away. He spent part of the time trying to get the world-weary ten-year old to talk to him. It was enough to make her agree to go out with him that first time. Two months later and she lingered, enjoying his company. He didn't even complain when Ella joined them on their third date because Layne made other plans and Jaime couldn't find a babysitter. Instead of letting her cancel, Drew brought over pizza, and they all watched a movie.

But it was just a fling, nothing serious. She didn't want to get in too deep and drag her daughter along with her. Being four years younger, Drew wasn't prepared for a ready-made family. She never asked him, but most twenty-five-year-old men she knew wanted to live their own lives, not raise another man's child.

Jaime pushed away those thoughts as she and Drew wandered around the store. They flipped through racks of old clothes and attempted to figure out what a few random knickknacks were. Jaime struggled to convince Drew to take off his hat and try on a bowler, but he wasn't having it.

"Are you really into this old stuff?" Drew asked as they reached a collection of antique instruments.

"I am." Jaime's heart soared when she thought about all of the old pieces that decorated her house. Even her furniture was vintage, bought from yard sales and thrift stores. She owned a few unique antique pieces as well. "All of these things once belonged to someone. Someone who lived and worked and dreamed in another time period." She plucked a guitar with no strings from its stand. "It's a way of time traveling, of being able to connect to history."

"You're Tristan in a dress." Drew chuckled, comparing her to his best friend and her office mate.

Jaime tipped her chin up as she smoothed her yellow, 1940's-inspired pencil skirt. "I'll take that as a compliment." She touched a tambourine with a hole in the center. "Anyway, take this, for instance. Who put the hole there? Did someone really play it that hard? Or did someone use it as a weapon?"

It jingled as Drew picked it up. "Maybe the player was pissed at her band mate?"

"Now you're getting the idea." She nudged him. "What do you think about an instrument as a decoration?"

"An instrument? Do you play?"

"No." She paused as the memory came back to her. "Well,

that's not totally true. My mother tried. Piano lessons twice a week when I was a kid. I hated every minute of it." She remembered the dread she felt when Mrs. Zhou from next door showed up for each and every torturous lesson. "All I can still play to this day is chopsticks."

"Then why an instrument?"

Jaime shrugged as she looked at the choices. "It's something different. I saw instruments hanging on the wall in a friend's house a few years ago and thought it looked amazing. Not the same boring paintings that everybody else has." She spent some time thinking about the idea. She measured and judged the walls in her living room, hunting for the right spot. Layne tried to talk her into a picture of an instrument, but it didn't have the same feel. A guitar or a violin would look amazing in the space on the wall.

Drew studied the selection, turning in a slow circle. He stopped when he faced the corner. "What about that one?" he breathed.

Jaime followed his line of sight. A small, orange violin leaned against the wall. It had dents and dings and a couple of the strings were missing. But something about it spoke to her. "I think we have a winner."

2

Something deep in his soul pulled at Drew when he set his eyes on the violin. He crossed to it, Jaime right behind him, and reached out to touch the ornately carved neck. It was smooth and cool under his hand. Jaime's fingers brushed his as she traced the remaining strings. A shock ran through his arm. He jerked away and studied his fingers.

"Pretty, isn't it?" Drew turned to see a woman with tanned skin, a long, brown braid, and bright blue-green eyes approach them. "This fiddle's only been here for about a month, just waiting for a new owner."

"Fiddle?" Jaime asked. "I thought it was a violin."

"It depends on how you play it, actually. And, we are in the mountains. Plus, the old gentleman who sold it to me said it was a fiddle." She walked around them and lifted the instrument. "Unfortunately, this fiddle doesn't have a bow to go with it, and it's missing a few strings." She plucked one of the remaining ones. "But with a little work and TLC, I think it might still play."

"What happened to it?" Drew stared at the fiddle as if he'd

never seen one before. Energy seemed to pulse off of it. The fine hairs on his arms stood at attention. He yearned to touch it again, which was weird because he'd never played an instrument before.

"Age, I suspect. It's more than a hundred years old."

Jaime's eyes widened. "Really?" She held out her hands, and the woman placed the fiddle into it. "It's such a beautiful piece."

The woman patted the neck. "The man who sold it to me said it once belonged to a pair of star-crossed lovers."

"Star-crossed lovers?" Drew refused to buy the story. He pictured a version of *Romeo and Juliet* with overalls, bare feet, and missing teeth. After all, he pegged the lady as the type who knew people loved a good tale to go along with the antique piece they were interested in.

"A poor man fell in love with a rich man's daughter, but no one approved of the match. They had to see each other in secret." The woman sighed. "The man swore the story was true. Of course, I'm not sure if it was true myself."

Jaime turned the fiddle over and studied the back. Compared to the front, it was smooth and untouched. She lifted the price tag. "Only twenty dollars?"

"I felt generous," the woman declared, flipping her braid over her shoulder.

"Can I see it?" Drew asked. Jaime gave the fiddle to him. When his fingers closed around the neck, it felt like it was supposed to be there. For a moment, he thought he could play it if he held a bow. But that was ridiculous. Drew had no idea how to play an instrument, much less a fiddle. He passed it back to Jaime. Their hands touched and another spark zinged up his arms. He met Jaime's eyes and realized she felt it, too.

"You're really going to do the instrument thing?" Layne

joined them, her arms full of clothes. She'd broken the moment.

Jaime smiled and nodded. "I am, and I think this is the right piece. Drew, what do you think?"

So many thoughts jumbled in his head. He regarded the fiddle again. Something about it made his nerves tingle. He touched the smooth surface, and a third electric shock passed through his arm. What was with all of the shocks? He didn't have a buildup of static electricity, did he? "It's nice."

"Good." Jaime passed the fiddle back to the woman. "I'll take it."

A couple of minutes later, Drew stood outside with Jaime and Layne. Layne held bags full of vintage clothes while Jaime carried her carefully wrapped fiddle.

"I can't wait to see the look on Ella's face when you show her that," Layne chuckled.

"Oh, she won't mind it." Jaime patted her new treasure.

"She'll roll her eyes."

"She's ten. She always rolls her eyes."

Drew ignored the weird feeling the antique instrument gave him and focused on the lovely woman in front of him. He had been in the ghost business for so long that every broken antique thing gave him chills. "So, want to grab a bite to eat?"

Jaime's expression was apologetic. "I can't. I have to pick up my daughter."

"That's cool. We can all grab something to eat."

"Not tonight." She clutched the fiddle. "It's girls' night."

"Okay. I can take a raincheck." On the outside, Drew tried to project an air of cool. On the inside, though, he wanted to kick a rock. But he understood that Ella came first. Jaime made that clear on their first date. He respected it.

"But if Layne wouldn't mind watching Ella, we can do

something tomorrow night." Jaime smiled sweetly at her friend.

"I suppose I could." Layne agreed. This time, the eyebrow wasn't arched, and Drew didn't feel like he was being judged. Maybe Layne accepted him and decided she liked him.

Layne shot him a narrow-eyed glance. Maybe not yet.

"Good. Then tomorrow at six?"

"I'm on board."

Ella, time for bed." Jaime poked her head into her daughter's room, hands on her hips. She cringed at how much she sounded like her mother.

"Mom!" The word came out as a groan with a long "o" in the middle. At ten, Ella was on the cusp of becoming a preteen, and Jaime had declined to deal with that yet. She wanted to hang onto her baby girl for as long as possible. "I gotta finish this game." She kept her eyes glued to her tablet, her thumbs flying over it.

Jaime tapped her fingernails on the doorjamb. "You can finish it tomorrow." She paused. "You have all day."

Ella lifted her head, Jaime's own light brown eyes looking back at her. "It's Friday night. Kelly doesn't have a bedtime."

Ah, the Kelly excuse. Jaime prepared for it. Ella always brought up her best friend when she didn't want to do something. "I'm not Kelly's mom, and you're not Kelly. Besides, it's already eleven." She stepped into the room. "Come on. Into bed."

Arguing was becoming a daily event. The script changed from time to time, but the roles stayed the same. Jaime asked Ella to do something. Ella created a thousand different reasons why she couldn't. Jaime worried about how much worse it might become as Ella got older.

Jaime cast her eyes heavenward. How did her mother ever get through this age with not one kid, but two? At twenty-nine, she considered herself too young to deal with this kind of thing, but she loved her daughter dearly. Even when she acted like a pain.

Ella groaned, but she saved the game and turned off the tablet. "You know, I'm not a baby anymore. Kelly gets to…"

"You're my baby, and I don't care what Kelly gets to do," Jaime interrupted. "To bed with you."

Ella crawled into the bed, and Jaime tucked her in.

"Good night, honey."

"Good night."

She kissed Ella's forehead before turning off the light and closing the door.

Jaime declared girl's night a success. They started off with pizza and a movie, but then Ella ran off to her room to do her own thing. That was Ella. Jaime knew her daughter liked spending time with her, but she also liked hanging out alone in her room. Jaime learned to deal with it, though she didn't completely understand it. While Jaime enjoyed hanging out with a crowd, Ella preferred her quiet time. Jaime shook her head as she walked away.

She made it halfway down the hall when cold pricked the back of her neck. A crisp wind raced down the hall. The chill ran through her bones and lifted her hair off her shoulders. Goosebumps broke out along her skin. Did she leave a window open?

Ella screamed. The piercing sound rang out through the house and stabbed Jaime's heart.

She rushed to her daughter's room. Fear clawed at her as she thought of every doomed scenario: Ella with a broken arm, Ella falling out of the window, someone breaking into Ella's room. Each imagined scene grew worse and worse. Jaime tried to think of positive things. It might be nothing.

Maybe Ella dropped something. Maybe she was overreacting. She did love the dramatic.

Jaime flew into Ella's room and came to an abrupt stop.

Ella sat on her bed, her knees drawn to her chin. Her entire body shook like a leaf. She stared at her closed closet door with wide eyes. Winter had come to her room, the icy air thick. Jaime wrapped her arms around herself, holding in a bit or warmth. She searched for an open window and found nothing.

"Ella?" Jaime crept to the bed.

"Mom. Look." Ella whispered as she pointed to her closet.

Jaime turned, and her blood chilled. She grabbed the bed post for support. For a rare moment, she had no words.

A white man, transparent in the moonlight, stood in the doorway. He was tall, lean, and wiry. He wore a hat that hinted at brown, covering shaggy, straight hair. Maybe it was blond or brown. Jaime couldn't tell. He wore a dingy work shirt with overalls. His eyes, she was too far away to see their color, fixed on Ella, a pleading look in them.

His feet, encased in scuffed work boots, didn't touch the ground.

Jaime swallowed and made herself push away from the bed. Her knees threatened to stop supporting her weight. She blinked a couple of times, not sure of what she saw. But her brain settled on an unbelievable word. Ghost. He looked exactly like a ghost.

All her life, she loved ghost stories. The creepier, the better. Especially if the story ended with blood dripping. Even her co-worker Tristan's experience with a ghost fascinated her. But she didn't fully believe his story about The White Lady who haunted his apartment building. It turned out her boss possibly killed her, and she killed him in return. When Tristan told her that, she recoiled at the idea.

This, however, was different. She separated herself from

the ghosts in the stories. This one floated in her daughter's bedroom.

"Please." His voice was soft, hard to hear. It sounded like it came through an old, crackling radio. "Please help me." A lilt of an accent tinged his words.

His image blinked out for a second. Jaime held up her hand to see if a projection showed on her skin. Maybe they were looking at a film or something. Was a neighbor playing a prank? She only saw her own smooth skin.

He stepped away from the closet and reached for Ella. "You have to hurry. You have to help."

Ella leapt from her bed and hid behind Jaime, like when she was a little girl. She wrapped her skinny, awkward arms around her mother's waist.

Jaime stood taller and thrust out her chin. Though she wanted to fall apart, she gathered her courage for her daughter. "Who are you?" She was surprised her voice held steady. "What do you want?" It took everything inside of her not to grab Ella and run.

Was she really talking to a guy she could see through?

She tried to turn on Ella's bedside lamp. The switch clicked, but the room stayed dark.

Ice started to form on the bed frame, creeping from one post to the post she held. She snatched her hand away, afraid it would freeze to the frame. The spider webs of ice twisted and intertwined as they covered the surface. She shivered.

The ghostly young man took another step toward them. "I don't have much time." He glanced over his shoulder. "Help me find my treasure." His accent sounded familiar. Scottish? Irish? Jaime couldn't quite place it.

"What treasure?" The question popped out. She blinked, wondering what she was doing. She stood in the middle of her daughter's bedroom talking to what appeared to be a ghost. Had she lost her mind?

Ghosts existed, according to her grandmother's stories from living in China. She grew up hearing stories about them, and they were never the good guys. Each of the stories told of the ways to keep them out of the house. At that moment, she didn't remember any of them and wished she had paid more attention.

She wracked her brain for an explanation. She'd made it back to her own room and was having the weirdest dream ever. She'd tripped and hit her head. But it didn't feel like a dream. It felt one hundred percent real. The cold pricked her skin, making her shiver. Her breath formed white clouds. Early November in Asheville gave a wintery vibe, but that was outside. Jaime kept the house toasty and warm.

The man's mouth opened to form a shocked circle. "I'm sorry. I'm sorry."

The bed, the dresser, and the desk shook as if they were in an earthquake. The floor rattled. A rumble filled Jaime's ears.

She clutched her daughter, shielding her with her body. A figurine of a ballerina flew off the dresser and smacked Jaime's shoulder. She gasped at the quick shot of pain. The figurine fell to the floor, breaking apart. Trophies, books, and dolls crashed with loud thumps. She fought to hold her balance as the room tumbled down around her and Ella.

The rumbling turned to a roar. It grew louder and louder like a train rushed through the room. The floor shook harder. The air around them changed to a biting whirlwind. It swirled,

keeping them rooted to their spot. It ripped Jaime's breath away.

"Mom!" Ella gripped tighter and shut her eyes.

"It's okay, baby. It's okay." Jaime held on for dear life.

A black shadow covered the moonlight reflecting across the wall. She shut her own eyes tightly. The room creaked as dark laughter filled it. Something cold and sharp raked along her skin.

Then as suddenly as it started, the chaos stopped. The floor stilled. The wind died. The roar quieted. Jaime opened one eye, then the other. She peered at Ella's closet and wall. The ghostly young man and the shadow were gone like they had never been there.

"I'm not sleeping in here!" Ella ran past her mother and out the door.

Jaime stood still as if her feet were rooted to the carpet. She took one breath and flipped the switch on the bedside lamp. Yellow light brightened the room. She breathed in again, her heart slowing to a normal rhythm. She moved one foot and then the other. She crossed to the area where the ghost had been. The area froze her skin, but that was it.

"What did you expect?" she muttered to herself. "Green slime?"

A loud, jaunty tune erupted from down the hall causing her to jump. The phone stopped ringing before it finished the song, and she heard Ella answer it. Jaime walked away from the closet door. She met her daughter in the hall.

Ella held out the cell phone. "It's Grandma. She said she's been trying to call, but the phone kept disconnecting."

Jaime brushed her hair off her shoulders. It was bound to be an interesting conversation.

3

A re you all right?" Her mother's worried voice bounced through the speaker.

Jaime closed and locked her door. "We're fine, Mom. Everyone's okay." She didn't elaborate because she knew her mother had perceived it.

"I saw it. I called a few minutes ago, but the phone rang and stopped. Over and over again. I wanted to warn you about the ghost."

"Thank you, Mom. I'm sorry. I guess we didn't hear it." Jaime lowered herself onto the bed. She inhaled slow breaths as her adrenaline eased off. Fight or flight warred inside her system. She cast a wary eye at her door.

"Come home now. Get out of that house." Jaime jumped at the command.

She glanced at Ella. Her daughter sat on the bed, knees to her chin and eyes on the door. "Did you see anything else?" At that moment, Jaime wished she had her mother's gift for seeing the future. Or any psychic gift at all, especially if it stopped a ghost.

As she understood it, her mother saw glimpses of a few

minutes ahead. Jaime recalled a day when her mother handed her an umbrella after the weather person declared a clear sky at the time and when her mother met her at the door asking why she'd done something before she opened her mouth. Her mother's clearest visions always seemed to center around Jaime and Ella, no matter how far away from Cary they lived.

"Only the ghost attacking."

"Do you see anything now?"

The other end was quiet for a moment. Jaime gripped the phone, her heart pounding. She glanced at the lock. Was it enough to keep a ghost out? Or did they travel through walls like the legends said?

"Nothing right now. I don't think he'll be back tonight."

Ella touched Jaime's shoulder. "Mom? Do I have to sleep in there?"

"No. You can stay with me tonight." She forced herself to smile, and deep inside, she was relieved that Ella made the suggestion. She didn't want her daughter out of her sight for the rest of the night.

"Jaime," her mother's voice cut in. "Make a line of salt along the bottom of every door and window. That should keep the ghost out for tonight."

Jaime paced away from the bed. "Salt my floor? Are you sure?"

"Yes. Do it."

She didn't believe the advice when she ended the call, but she dashed down the stairs and grabbed the salt. When she returned, she poured lines under all the doors and windows. She climbed onto her bed and rubbed her upper arms, unable to get warm.

A ghost was in her house. A ghost! It was impossible! But she had seen him with her own eyes.

"Well, Jaime, people say psychics aren't real, and you

know they are," she said to herself. Not only had she seen her mother predict the future and Tristan describe the past, but her own daughter had a talent, too.

She thought Ella's gift was the most amazing of all. She found things, always knowing exactly where they hid. It started right after her tenth birthday. She located all sorts of knickknacks and misplaced items in the house. Jaime tested it once by hiding her keys when she knew Ella sat in her room. She knocked on her daughter's door and asked for her help. Ella, without even thinking about it, hunted them down in less than a minute.

But ghosts were another matter entirely. Were people able to hang on to this world after they died? And even more pressing, could a dead person shake furniture and floors and call up wind? Or freeze things? How? The more she thought about it, the more it scared her to the bone.

Drew would know. The idea popped into her head out of nowhere. Of course. She was dating a ghost hunter. He bragged about getting ghosts to go away all the time. She picked up her phone and pulled up his number. Her thumb hovered over the call button. It was midnight. She couldn't call him out of the blue. But if she were dealing with a break-in, she wouldn't hesitate to call the police. Pressing her lips together, Jaime hit the button.

C ome on, baby. Work for me." Drew stood in the middle of his tiny basement apartment living room. His new machine, shaped like a black ray gun, rested sleek and cool in his left hand. His Ghost Disruptor! He studied the smooth lines. Was Ghost Disruptor really the right name? Ghost Destroyer sounded good, but it didn't really destroy ghosts. Ghost Scrambler rolled off the tongue, but it also put him in the mood for eggs. No, that sounded ridiculous. He chose to stick with Ghost Disruptor. He could change it later.

It was too bad no ghosts haunted his apartment. He wanted to test it and make sure it worked. He needed to know if it broke them apart like he planned. Instead, he settled for messing with the regular energy. If the disruptor caused his lights to blink, then it might cause a ghost to let go of all the energy it held. He held his breath and shoved a sixteen-amp battery into the handle. He aimed the disruptor at the nearest lamp and pressed the red power button with his forefinger.

The disruptor whirred with a hum that grew louder, ringing in his ears. A row of green lights on top of the barrel lit up one by one. When the final one flicked on, the lamp's light blinked off for a moment. Then the other lights in the room began to blink on and off as well.

Excitement bubbled in Drew's chest. "Yes!" He pumped his fist in the air. "Finally!"

But his happiness was short-lived. The small gun heated, burning his palm. He tossed it to the floor with a yelp. All the tiny lights flared before the whole thing popped and shut off. Smoke floated out of the tip of the barrel.

"Dammit." Drew touched a finger to it, but the metal was still hot. He sighed and dropped onto his couch. "Looks like it's back to the drawing board." He rubbed his chin. "What am I missing?"

A tinny version of "Iron Man" played from the side table. Drew peered at his phone, surprised to see Jaime's name on the display. He answered without hesitation.

"Couldn't wait for tomorrow night, huh?"

"Drew, can you come over?" Her voice shook.

He let go of the joke. "Are you okay? What's wrong?"

"A ghost attacked Ella."

He didn't hesitate. "I'll be right there."

It took him ten minutes to fly across town to Jaime's two-bedroom bungalow. He made sure he packed an electromagnetic field detector before he left. The tiny machine would detect the ghost's presence before he could. He didn't want to bring all the cameras and tape recorders and other electronic paraphernalia that he usually brought to a job, but he did want to be prepared. He cursed the fact his disruptor didn't work yet.

Jaime paced on her porch, bundled in a heavy coat. Her breath made white plumes of smoke. She raced down the stairs when he pulled into her driveway.

"Can you make it go away?" she asked as he got out of the car. "Bust him or something?"

"Whoa, slow down." He palmed the EMF detector, a small, black machine with several different colored lights on top of it. "What's going on?"

As they walked into the house, Jaime described a male ghost wearing a hat and overalls and asking Ella for his treasure.

"He talked to her?" Drew latched onto that detail. In the year he'd worked at Restless Spirits, he only learned of a handful of ghosts who talked to the living. He saw a couple of them himself. The White Lady had been one of them, but she only spoke to Tristan and her victims.

"Yes. That's what you're focusing on?" Jaime's eyes widened.

Her words put the brakes on his mounting excitement. "I'm sorry. You're right. Is she okay?" He had to remember that her daughter was involved. Her ten-year-old daughter.

"Yeah." Jaime's tense shoulders eased as she loosened her grip on her T-shirt. "She's sleeping in my room with salt covering every door and window."

"Good thinking."

"My mom's advice." Jaime squared her shoulders. "Now, how do we get rid of him?"

Drew showed her the EMF detector. "We have to search for him first and find out why he's here."

Jaime's brow wrinkled. "You can't just make him go away?"

"This isn't *Ghostbusters*. I can't suck him up into a ghost trap and take him to an Ecto Containment Unit, and believe me, I've tried to make one before." He sighed. Her face fell. He was letting her down, and he hated himself for it. "You said you saw him in Ella's room, right?" He headed for the stairs. "Maybe he'll reappear and tell me what he wants." He hoped so, anyway. If the ghost was a talker, he might be able to help him depart within the week and not have to call in the team.

Jaime lowered her shoulders. "I know this isn't a movie. I just want Ella to be safe."

Drew took her small hand in his. "She will be. I promise."

Jaime led him to Ella's room. He stopped her as she reached for the light switch.

"You can see a ghost better in the dark," he explained.

"Okay." She didn't seem convinced, but she stepped back.

Drew faced the darkened room. A little bluish light filtered in through the window thanks to the streetlamp outside. It formed a small rectangle on the opposite wall. He took a deep breath and turned on the EMF detector. It crackled a bit before settling into a steady hum. Then it purred like a kitten.

He crossed to the closet door and held up the detector. The lights stayed steady. No lingering energy to cause the lights to move or to make a high-pitched whine. He stepped away from the area and walked a slow circle around the room. Nothing. Not a peep. Whatever entity had appeared in

Ella's room, it left no trace. Drew turned off the machine. He shook his head.

"I'm not picking up anything," he said.

Jaime flicked a switch, and light flooded the room. "He was here. I swear he was."

"I believe you. But he's gone now."

She crossed her arms, blowing out a breath. "Maybe he won't come back."

"Maybe."

He followed her back down the stairs and into the living room. Setting the EMF detector down, he wrapped his arms around her. "How are you doing?"

"Better, but I feel like an idiot." She snuggled into him, resting her head on his chest. "I won't blame you if you think I'm crazy."

"Hot, yes. Amazing, yes. But never crazy." He kissed her forehead. "I'm not giving up. Come down to the office tomorrow. Tell the rest of the team what you told me. We can bring in all the equipment and the psychics and see what we can find out."

She smiled up at him. "Psychics, plural? I thought McKenna was the only one. Did Tristan finally decide to work with you? He was on the fence last time I talked to him."

"Yeah. He still isn't completely in control yet, but he's trying. He's at least started to accept his gift instead of trying to fight it." Drew tucked a strand of hair behind her ear. He loved the feel of her in his arms. "But I don't want to talk about my best friend while I'm trying to get with my girlfriend."

"Girlfriend?" Jaime's brows shot up. "Are we labeling this? I thought we were just having fun." She pulled away, leaving emptiness in her wake.

Drew blinked, his heart sinking. He hadn't expected an

abrupt reaction. He wiggled the bill of his cap as he shifted away. He worried that he pushed too hard. "I didn't mean to freak you out. I thought since we'd been on several dates, planning another one, and I really like you, that we'd reached that level." He rubbed his hands on his jeans, feeling like an idiot.

The awkward silence stretched. Drew questioned whether he should leave or not.

Jaime paced around to the other side of a nearby winged armchair, placing the piece of furniture between them. She ran a hand over the curved back. "I don't know. I have to think about Ella."

"Ella's great. She doesn't say much to me, but she's great." He told her the truth. He admired Jaime's daughter, but Ella stuck to one-syllable answers each time he spoke to her. She also narrowed her eyes at him when he took Jaime out on a date, like Layne. "Does Ella hate me? Is that why you want to break up?"

"Break up?" Jaime straightened. "I don't want to break up. Do you want to break up?"

"No!" Drew ran around the chair. "I thought...you said... I'm confused."

"Me, too." Jaime draped her arms around his neck. "Maybe I'm not ready for the word 'girlfriend' yet. Is that okay?"

"Yeah, yeah. We'll come up with a better word." He pulled her closer. "How about 'Really Hot Friend'?"

A smile spread across her amazing mouth. "I can handle that." Her cheeks pinked. "Why don't I make us some coffee? I feel safer with you here."

"I love coffee."

Jaime kissed him quick on the mouth before walking into the kitchen. He felt the goofy grin on his face and tried to suppress it. Goofy grins did not convey manliness. He was supposed to smolder. A protector smoldered, right? He bounced a little as he looked around the room. His eyes landed on the antique fiddle above her couch.

"Hey, you hung the fiddle already," he called.

"I couldn't wait when I got it home," she answered. "Ella said she thought it was lame." She chuckled. "What does she know?"

Drew lifted his hand and touched one of the strings. A sharp edge pricked his finger. He yanked his hand away as he jumped at the quick, sharp pain. The tip of his forefinger bled. "Hey, got a Band-Aid?"

"Yeah. Top drawer in the downstairs bathroom."

He sucked on the wound, turning in the direction of the bathroom. Ice cold air prickled his skin. The fine hair on his arms stood at attention. He pulled his finger out of his mouth and lifted his head. A dark shadow slinked across the wall as the lights flickered. A deep laugh echoed. The floor under his feet rumbled.

He grabbed the arm of the couch as his heart jumped into his throat. He breathed out small, white circles. Something sharp pricked the back of his neck. He clapped a hand on it. When he whirled around, nothing was there.

All of the activity stopped as suddenly as it started. The air warmed, the lights remained on, and the shadow and the laugh vanished into thin air.

4

Jaime concentrated on facts and logics as she worked through the ghost situation. Freaking out about the unexplained wouldn't help anybody. She handled things by reviewing the facts. When she found out she was pregnant, she read every book on the subject she could found. When she wanted to go back to school because working at Target did not fit her end goal, she researched every college in the state, searching for the best program.

She planned to deal with the ghost in the same way.

Jaime spent Saturday at a table in the Pack Memorial Library with her laptop and books on Asheville's local history while Ella hung out at a friend's house. She included a couple of books on local ghost stories in her stack.

The ghost stories didn't offer much help. They focused on the Pink Lady at the Grove Park Inn, probably Asheville's most famous ghost. Other stories centered on ghosts in town, and one talked about the graveyard found behind an old high school. She even found a mention about The White Lady of Hidden Forest Apartments. But nothing about her house, her neighborhood, or even the land it was built on.

She pored through the local history books, but the authors didn't include violent deaths or ghost legends. Some of them read as dry as dust.

Jaime slammed one of the books shut. A nearby older lady at a computer shushed her and narrowed her eyes.

After a harrowing weekend of Ella sleeping in her room with salt lining the bottom of the windows and the doors, Jaime had reached her wits' end. On Drew's advice, she brought the case to his team at Restless Spirits, Inc. She didn't count on hiring a group of ghost hunters when she laid out her budget for the month, but if they found a way to make the ghost leave, she'd produce the money.

On Monday morning, she settled at a round conference table in the back of the Restless Spirits' office on Haywood Street.

She studied the four full-time members of paranormal investigation team, and Tristan Johnson, her officemate who worked with the team part time. She had met Aaron and Tabitha Lawson, the owners, and McKenna at The White Lady's grave so no one acted like a stranger.

Tabitha sat to her left at the round conference table, a short, curvy woman with a spiky cap of purple and blonde hair. Her bright blue eyes regarded Jaime as she tapped her fingers on the table.

Aaron, a tall man with short dark hair and a brooding medium brown eyes, sat next to her. He leaned back, rested one leg on top of the other, and rocked.

McKenna and Tristan sat on the right side, a pen and paper in McKenna's hands. Her long brown hair fell in waves past her ivory shoulders, and her blue eyes sparkled. Tristan's golden skin was a contrast to her as he shook out his black curls and rubbed his green eyes.

Then there was Drew. He sat next to her, a hand resting on her back. She and Ella weren't alone in this, and that gave her courage. He adjusted his Blue Devils baseball cap and gave her an encouraging smile. "Whenever you're ready."

"I don't know where to start. Never thought I'd be here talking about my haunted house." Jaime fidgeted with the end of her ruffled shirt.

"That's okay. Drew said your daughter is involved." McKenna covered Jaime's other hand with her own. "You're nervous. Is it okay if I help you feel calmer?"

Jaime swallowed. "You can do that?"

"Sure can. But I won't unless you say it's okay."

Jaime nodded. McKenna smiled as a sense of ease settled over her. Jaime's muscles loosened, and her whole body relaxed. Her nerves seemed to melt away.

"Wow. Tristan said you were good, but I didn't know how good. Thank you."

"Told you," Tristan said as he draped an arm across McKenna's shoulders.

McKenna squeezed her hand. "You're welcome. Now, go ahead. We're listening."

Jaime took a deep breath and plunged into the story. It tumbled out of her, easier than last time. She didn't know whether to thank McKenna's influence or the fact she'd recounted the events before. She told them about Ella's scream and the ghost standing in front of the closet doorway. She included all the details.

"What did he look like?" Aaron was bent over a notebook, his pen scribbling across the paper.

"Transparent. We could see right through him, like he was a hologram." Jaime twirled the end of her ponytail as she thought back to Friday night. Had it really only been a few days ago? "He was young, wearing a pair of overalls and a wide-brimmed hat. He had a work shirt on underneath, like they wore in the turn of the century." The history nerd inside of her kicked in. "I'd say he was from the mountains, maybe the Great Smoky Mountains or the Blue Ridge. He appeared to be from any time period between the late 1800s and the early 1900s, but I couldn't say for sure."

"Did he talk to you?" McKenna asked. Jaime held on to her like a lifeline.

"Yeah. He said, 'Help me.' His accent wasn't southern. I think it had an Irish or Scottish lilt." Her brow furrowed. "Maybe British." Jaime took a deep breath. "He talked to Ella."

Aaron's knee bounced up and down. "That doesn't sound like a threat."

"No, I guess not. The whole room started shaking, and wind blew inside my house. A ballerina figurine hit me here." She pointed to the back of her shoulder. "There's a small bruise, but that's it. Ella wasn't hurt." She thanked her lucky stars for that.

Tabitha tapped the end of her pen against the desk. "Why would a ghost ask for help before attacking?"

Jaime shrugged. "I wish I knew." Right then, another detail popped into her mind. "Wait. He did say something else. He said, 'I'm sorry,' before everything went crazy."

Aaron lifted a brow. "That's new. It sounds like this ghost is aware of what he's doing."

"I don't think a malicious ghost would apologize. Most of them are full of anger and hate," McKenna said.

"Unless he can't control it." Tabitha suggested. "Is there anything else, Ms. Liu?"

"Please, call me Jaime." Jaime breathed in more calming, warm air. "As soon as the chaos started, it stopped. He was gone. But my daughter was shaking so badly, we didn't get any sleep that night. Drew stayed the whole time on the couch."

"Drew, did you see anything?" Aaron straightened as he sipped a cup of coffee.

"The EMF detector didn't pick up anything in the room,

and he didn't make another appearance for the rest of the night." Jaime notice him dart a quick glance her way. "But something happened in the living room while Jaime was in the kitchen before she went back to bed."

He saw something, and he didn't tell her? Jaime pulled her hand away from McKenna's as she faced Drew. "You kept something from me?"

"I didn't want to worry you."

"Worry me? You were there to see the ghost. If you saw him and didn't tell me, what's the point?" Jaime's shoulders tensed and all of McKenna's calming effect was ruined. Thoughts spun around in her head. What if the incident he hadn't told her about had harmed Ella? She trembled with the effort to not yell at him.

"Drew," Aaron interrupted. "Spill it."

"I was in the living room looking at the fiddle I helped Jaime pick out yesterday. It's a nice piece." He raked a hand through his hair. "Anyway, the temperature dropped, the lights flickered, and I saw a shadow move across the wall. The furniture shook, too. Someone laughed. And then it was over."

Jaime let some of her anger go. "I didn't feel or hear anything in the kitchen."

"So it's not limited to Ella's room?" Tabitha wrinkled her brow.

"I didn't see the ghost at all, but the shaking, the lights, and the cold were all the same."

"Well, since a kid's safety is involved, I want to take care of this as soon as possible." Aaron closed his notebook with a definitive snap. "McKenna, Tristan, I want to know everything about that house you can dig up. Who lived there, when, how long? Everything."

"I've already started looking into some things," Jaime glanced around the table. "I haven't really found much yet."

"I'd like to see what you've got," Tristan sat forward.

"That's not a problem."

Aaron raised an eyebrow. "Tristan, you up for trying to fill in the blanks?"

He exchanged a look with McKenna. "I can try."

"You don't have to." Jaime remembered the few times she saw him pass out from visions in their office.

"Thanks for worrying, but I'll be okay."

Aaron continued down his checklist. "Tabitha, you and Drew start gathering the equipment." He then turned his attention to Jaime. Unprepared for his intense gaze, she jumped to attention. "How soon can we set up in your house?"

"As soon as you want to." Jaime knew the relief running through her wasn't from McKenna this time. "When do most people do it?"

"Usually on the weekends, but we can set up whenever you're ready for us," Tabitha answered, her tone gentler than her husband's.

"Then, tonight? Tomorrow?" It happened so fast. Could the ghost really be gone by the end of the week? Jaime dared to hope.

"I think we can make it happen tomorrow night." Aaron stood. Chairs scraped against the floor as everyone followed his lead.

Jaime blinked at everyone. "That's it?"

"That's it." McKenna nodded to the door. "I'd actually like to drop by sometime tonight and talk to Ella. Get her take on the situation. Is that okay?" The shorter woman hustled to the desk in front of the glass door.

"Yeah." Jaime ran to catch up with her. "Yeah. Ella's a little shy at first, but I think she'll feel better knowing you're there to help."

"Good. I can't wait to meet her." McKenna indicated the

chair across from her. She brought up a calendar on her desktop.

As Jaime settled on a time with her, control seemed to return to her. She had a plan, a purpose, and something more permanent than salt on her floor. After she and McKenna scheduled the time and finalized the details, she met Drew at the door.

"Walk you to your car?" He pushed open the glass door, and the small bell above it jingled.

"Thank you." She buttoned her coat, stepping out in the frigid air. She popped her pocket book on her shoulder and stuffed her hands into her pockets. "Is this normal?"

"What? Cold temperatures in autumn?" Drew rubbed his hands together before jamming them into the pockets of his coat. He hunched his shoulders against the bracing wind as they headed up the hill to the parking garage behind the Pack Library.

"No. The way you and your team make people feel comfortable, even when they're talking about the craziest things." Her boots clicked on the sidewalk. "You've got to know ghosts and hauntings aren't everyday occurrences, right?"

"Well, they're every day for us, but I know what you mean." Drew bobbed his head. "If they turned up as often as people claimed, we'd make bank." He grinned at her. "Seriously, though, making people comfortable is a part of the job. We're not here to judge; we're here to help. And people need a place like ours when no one else believes them."

Jaime lifted her face to the morning sunshine, wishing for the heat of June. "Ghosts are a part of my culture, you know. I grew up hearing about how this auntie saw this ghost or how that auntie swore the ghost of her dead husband watched over her. But I don't think I ever really believed in them. Not until Tristan faced his two months ago. And I never saw her."

"I grew up with a few ghost stories of my own, mostly from my mom's side. When your family comes from the south, you're bound to hear a lot of tall tales." He chuckled. "My favorite came from my uncle. He insisted a ghost haunted the little room under the stairs when he was a kid. My mom said she never saw it."

Jaime took a shaky breath. "But this one isn't a tall tale. This one was real and came after my daughter." She pushed away the fear and let the anger simmering underneath come to the surface. "I'll do anything to keep her safe."

Drew stopped and touched Jaime's chin. She leaned into his warm caress against the icy air. "So will I. You have my word."

<hr>

Ella stood at the top of the stairs. She crossed her arms and glared at the door at the end of the hall. The door leading to her room. She'd returned to it since the ghost first showed up, but she never stayed long. Dash in, dash out. She acted a baby about this whole thing, and it embarrassed her. It was just a creepy transparent dead guy. No big deal.

She didn't need this whole ghost thing on top of everything else going on in her life. Renee Lawson, one of the popular girls at school, made it her life's mission to ruin Ella's school year. Ella hadn't told her mother because ten-year olds don't tattle, but Renee pulled her hair, dumped her bookbag into the trash can, and called her all sorts of terrible names. Names she refused to think about. She even backed Ella into a corner of the girl's bathroom once. Thank goodness her best friend Kelly walked in at that moment and helped Ella fight Renee off.

Her freaky talent for finding things unnerved her. It started right after her birthday. Objects sang to her. Well, not really sang, but they played their own vibrations, like soft music only Ella could hear. She tried to explain it to her mom once, but it all came out in a confusing jumble. Her mother said her talent was cool, but Ella knew she said that because she was her mother. Moms were supposed to think everything was cool.

The new guy her mom dated posed another problem. Drew. He didn't seem so bad, but Ella knew he tried too hard. He'd stuck around so far, butting into her time with her mom. However, she knew he'd leave like all the others. He'd get bored with having a kid hang around. They all did. And neither she nor her mom had any time for that.

Her final concern was Ryan Marion. He sat next to her in class. Ryan. Marion. He was the cutest, most adorable boy in school, and she sounded like a complete idiot anytime she stood near him. Her last great conversation with him involved asking him if he needed a pencil. How stupid!

No, she juggled too much stuff in her life to deal with a stalkery ghost.

She squared her shoulders and sucked in a deep breath. She was ten-years old, not a baby anymore. And she needed her math book that she'd left in her room that morning.

Ella flipped on the overhead light. She eyed the closet as she crept into the room. No sign of the ghost at all. Nothing but the poster of her favorite pop band smiling at her from the door. Nothing to be afraid of. She'd dash in and dash out. No problem.

She scurried across the room to her desk, grabbed the hefty yellow book, and scurried back.

A creak caught her attention. She froze before she reached the exit. She knew she shouldn't have come in there at night.

"Help me." The ghost hovered in front of her closet, arm outstretched. "Please help me find my treasure." His voice cracked with the same static, but this time it sounded like he was everywhere.

The overhead light flickered, and the room grew colder.

Holding her breath, Ella ran for the door. It slammed shut in her face. She dropped her book and grabbed the knob, but it wouldn't turn.

"Mom!" She banged on it. "Mom!"

The room plunged into darkness. Ella whirled, her eyes adjusting to the faint light outside her window.

A deep laugh bounced off every wall. It wasn't full of static like the other voice. It rang out menacing and clear. A black shape formed next to her, almost out of nowhere. It opened two red eyes, bright and terrifying. It surrounded her, smoky and ice cold. She smelled rotten eggs and tried not to gag.

Something solid grabbed her arm and squeezed. Sharp pinpricks dug into her skin.

"Let go!" Ella pulled against the grip, screaming. She turned and kicked out. Her foot flew through a dark shape. Icy air pushed through her jeans. A deep laugh echoed around the room.

The shape tightened around her, stealing all of the air. Pain ran up and down her arm, from her wrist to her shoulder. Cold, cold, cold.

"Let me go!"

"Ella? Open the door!" *Mom!*

"I can't."

The doorknob rattled. "Ella!"

Ella screamed again.

5

The black shadow blocked out every bit of light as it surrounded her. Red eyes bored into her. Ella's heart thudded against her ribs. She felt lightheaded, and her lungs lost air. She shivered as the cold slinked along her skin. But she fought, screamed, and kicked at the black shape.

"Go away! Go away! Leave me alone!"

Wet, warm drops trickled down her arm. It hurt so much. Tears streamed down her face and everything blurred.

"What do you want?"

Something heavy banged against the door. "Ella!" Mom again. "Drew, McKenna, help me get this door open." Heavy banging continued.

"Ella?" A man's voice came through the door. *Drew!* "Hang in there. I'm coming." Something hit the door with a thundering boom.

But the sound didn't register. Ella stumbled to the side, her attention no longer on her Mom and Drew. Her kicks and screams slowed down. Everything felt like it moved in slow motion. Cold engulfed her. If she laid down, she knew she'd feel better. She wasn't scared anymore, only tired. So tired.

"I'll destroy everything of his," the deep voice hissed. "Everything!"

All of a sudden, the black smoke jerked its claws out of her arm. "You're not his," it hissed. "But I'll take you anyway. You won't be able to help him."

Right when Ella's head rolled back, a ghostly white light broke through the dark smoke. Ice prickled along her skin as something else touched her injured arm. But it didn't bring pain, only a light, chilly touch. No claws, no scratches.

"No!" She heard the static voice. Ella lifted her eyes to see the ghost standing between her and the black smoke. She saw his back as he shifted between them. He towered over her. His blondish-brown hair stuck out from under his wide-brimmed hat. He smelled like freshly mowed grass. Ella started. Did ghosts smell? "No!" He took a step forward.

"You're not strong enough," the black shape growled. "She'll be mine, like all the others."

The ghost pulled Ella away from the door. "She's not yours." He nodded behind them. "She belongs to her."

The door burst open and swung so hard it hit the wall. Salt sailed through the air, landing on Ella. Both the shadow and the ghost broke apart. They disappeared, leaving wisps behind.

The light came back on as the room warmed. Ella rubbed her injured arm. Pain throbbed from the bloody marks left from the claws. She swayed on her feet and dropped into her mother's arms.

Jaime paced the living room floor. She rubbed at her face as she tried to steady her breathing. Every few minutes, she checked the couch to make sure her daughter was still there and still alive. After she pulled Ella from her room, she cleaned the red scratch marks on Ella's arm and bandaged it. Ella hadn't stirred for the past thirty minutes.

McKenna sat next to Ella. "Are you sure I can't help you?" She addressed her question to Jaime.

"No. I'm fine. I need to work this anger out." Jaime stopped as her throat started to close again. Tears burned behind her eyes, and she willed them to stay away.

Heavy footsteps trotted down the stairs, and Drew appeared around the corner. He held up the silent, dark EMF detector. "Nothing left. No trace of anything."

Jaime resumed her pacing, but only got a couple of footsteps in. Drew stood in front of her.

"How is she?" he asked.

"Still not moving." She turned on her heel and headed for the kitchen. She needed to do something, anything. She had to think. "I don't understand why this keeps happening." She ran her hands through her hair. "Where did these ghosts come from?" Ghosts. Plural. She had seen two different entities when Drew managed to get the door open. One tried to hurt her daughter, the other seemed like he fought to protect her. "Why do they want Ella?"

"I don't know. That's what we need to find out." Drew kept pace with her.

Once in the kitchen, Jaime grabbed her favorite tea kettle, the one shaped like an elephant, and filled it with water. She didn't drink tea that often, usually only when she or Ella were sick or when stress bogged her down. Right now, both reasons qualified. The smell and taste always helped her relax and made her think of home.

"I want both of them gone." Her declaration broke the small silence between them. "I want Ella safe."

"She will be." Drew took the kettle from her before it overflowed with water.

Jaime huffed as water dribbled over her hand. Her focus remained on her daughter.

"Ella is my whole world." She met his soft hazel eyes. "She wasn't part of my life plan, but when she came along, nothing else mattered. I wanted nothing more than to give her everything." A warm tear slid down her cheek, followed by a few more. Jaime wiped her eyes as Drew's face blurred. "What if I can't protect her from this?" Her voice hitched on the last word.

"Jaime, she's awake," McKenna called.

"Mom?"

Jaime raced into the living room, the idea of tea forgotten. "I'm here." She held back the rest of her tears, trying to be strong.

Ella's brown eyes darted from her Mom to McKenna and then landed on Drew. "What happened?" They widened. "Where are the ghosts?"

"Gone for now." McKenna rubbed her good arm. "The salt will keep them away for a while."

"You stopped them?" Ella asked.

"For now. Can you tell us everything that went on in your room?"

Ella swallowed and pulled herself into a sitting position. She winced, and Jaime swore she felt her pain. Ella told them about going to get her math book and how she planned to make it fast. Then how the black shadow, which smelled and felt more like smoke, appeared.

Her brow furrowed as she tried to remember every detail.

"He said he wanted to destroy everything of his. I wasn't his, but he wanted to kill me anyway."

"Oh, God." Quick anger flashed through Jaime, fighting with the fear.

McKenna touched her arm.

"Did the ghost say that?" Drew knelt down beside Jaime.

"No." Ella shook her head. "The black smoke did. It had a deep voice, like a guy. Deeper than yours." She pressed her lips together. "I think the first ghost tried to protect me."

"Do you know who the smoke was talking about?" McKenna asked.

"No."

Ella took a shaky breath and her eyes landed on the colorful socks McKenna wore. "Is that Wonder Woman on your socks?"

McKenna pointed a toe with a chuckle. "It sure is."

A slow smile crept across Ella's mouth. "Cool."

She pointed at Ella's own socks. "I see you have constellations on yours."

"It's the Big Dipper and the Little Dipper."

"Two of my favorites."

Jaime breathed a sigh of relief at the exchange. Ella sounded like Ella again, which meant she was going to be all right. But Jaime knew they couldn't stay in the house that night. Even with the salt blocking all the entrances in her room. Whatever these ghosts wanted, it involved Ella.

McKenna exchanged a glance with Drew before turning her attention back to the girl. "Ella, can I ask you something weird?" She placed her hands on her lap.

"I guess." Ella shrugged.

"Do you sometimes know things others don't know?"

A wary look came into Ella's eyes. "What do you mean?"

Warning bells went off in Jaime's head. Ella didn't like talking about her talent, and she didn't want her daughter to feel like she had to tell other people about it. "What does this have to do with anything?" She asked the question sharper than she intended.

"Do you think this is like Tristan and The White Lady?" Drew asked.

"What? What are you talking about?"

"The White Lady latched onto Tristan because he was psychic," McKenna explained. "She attacked me for the same reason."

"I don't understand." Jaime settled on the couch next to her daughter. She knew about Tristan's ability to see the past, but never made the connection with the ghost.

"It's a theory. There's no proof. But we think psychics might give off more energy than non-psychics. A ghost might be able to sense that and zero in on it." McKenna smiled at Ella. "If Ella has a psychic power, then that might explain why the ghosts chose her."

Ella narrowed her eyes. "Are you psychic?"

"I am." McKenna nodded. "I'm an empath."

Ella wrinkled her brow again. "A what?"

"An empath. A psychic who can feel your emotions."

Ella let that statement sink in. "That's not a real thing." The words slipped out before Ella could stop them.

"Ella." Jaime nudged her. "Be nice."

"That's okay." McKenna waved her hand. "People older than Ella have said worse to me." She rested a hand on Ella's injured arm. "Can I try something?"

"Okay." Ella's face held the wary look.

McKenna closed her eyes and stayed quiet for a moment. Then Ella's eyebrows shot up.

"Ella?"

"My arm doesn't hurt as bad."

McKenna opened her eyes. "But mine now aches." She

rubbed her own arm. "It'll start hurting again in a few minutes, though. I'm sorry about that."

"It's okay. I guess this means you're kind of like Grandma."

"Grandma?"

"My mom can see flashes of the immediate future and always tells me if it involves Ella or me," Jaime said.

"Ah, I see. Now back to the original question. What about you, Ella?"

Ella looked at Jaime, who nodded. "It's okay. She's an empath. She'll understand. You can trust her."

Ella swallowed. "I can find things. Lost things." She nodded to Drew. "He left his keys upstairs." She cocked her head to the right. "On my dresser."

Drew jumped up and padded his pockets. "Excuse me, ladies. I have to check something." He dashed up the stairs. Within a few minutes, he was back with the car keys in his hand. "She was right. And now, the whole treasure-finding thing makes sense."

"You think the ghost knows I can find things?" Ella asked.

"I think so." Drew stuffed the keys into his pocket.

"But that still doesn't explain where he came from or the black smoke. Or how to get rid of them." Jaime tossed her hands into the air, defeated.

"Well, we know the ghost wants his treasure. Maybe it's buried in the house?" McKenna stood. "Ella, can you try to find it?"

"I don't think that's a good idea." The clock on the wall read nine o'clock. "Ella has school tomorrow, and I have a room to salt again."

"Mom, I can do it." Ella threw the blanket off her and swung her feet to the floor. Her eyes brightened as color seeped back into her cheeks. "This house is filled with old stuff. Maybe one of them is the treasure." She jumped to her feet, but she didn't get far. She swayed before dropping back down to the couch.

"It's a definite no for tonight." Jaime slashed her hand in the air. Treasure, an insistent ghost, and murderous sentient black smoke was enough for tonight. Plus, her daughter stood in the middle of it. She reached her limit.

"But Mom…"

"No buts. It's about your bedtime."

Ella groaned and fell back on the couch.

Jaime walked McKenna and Drew to the door. "Thank you for your help tonight. I know you didn't plan to rescue my daughter."

"No thanks needed. We'll be back tomorrow night with all the equipment. Then we can see what we're really up against." McKenna patted Drew on the shoulder. "I'll see you tomorrow." With a knowing smile, she left.

"I can stay again tonight if you want. Your couch is pretty comfortable." He tucked a strand of dark hair behind her ear.

"You don't have to. I'll pour salt along the doors and windows in the bedroom, and as long as Ella doesn't go into her room, I think we'll be okay. I'll see you tomorrow."

"Okay." Drew rubbed her arms before leaning in and giving her a quick kiss.

The touch zinged all the way down to her toes.

"Call me if you need me." He then walked out the door. For the first time in a long time, the house felt almost empty.

6

The red marks on Ella's arm symbolized failure for Jaime. She hadn't reached her daughter fast enough. She shouldn't have let Ella go into her room alone. What she saw clutching her daughter had not been the ghost. A dark, sinister shadow hurt her child, and she swore its eyes glowed red.

Why did the attack happen after a couple of days of nothing? Ella had walked back in her room several times since the first ghost sighting. It didn't make any sense, and Jaime sensed her grip on reality slip.

In the light of day, the scariness diminished. The sun streamed in through the windows, and all was quiet in Ella's room. Ella, however, refused to go in. Jaime didn't blame her. She remained well away from it, too.

The marks on Ella's arm faded overnight, no longer as red or jagged. They left behind four tiny scars.

After talking her daughter into going to school, Jaime sailed into the office at Blackwood College with a can of Mountain Dew in her hand. Thank goodness she scheduled the full investigation for that night. Drew and his team would be there with all of his equipment, but Jaime wanted to make sure a certain person arrived. And she hoped he would use his ability to help her. She hit her hand on Tristan's desk.

He looked up, surprised. "Jaime?"

"Are you going to be at my house tonight? With the rest of the team?"

Tristan leaned back in his chair and blinked at her. "I was planning on it." His expression softened. "How's Ella?"

Jaime blinked, her drink bobbling in her hand. "She's better. How did you know?"

"I haven't turned into a mind reader." He held up his hands, palms out. "McKenna told me."

Jaime relaxed. "That makes sense." She drank some of her Mountain Dew, taking a moment to regroup. "Now, about tonight. Will you just be researching, or can I ask you a personal favor?"

"What is it?" He narrowed his green eyes.

"Find out what the hell is in my house."

"We plan to, but it might take a while." He raked black curls out of his eyes. "When the team goes in, they're thorough. I've learned a lot while working with them."

"I know that, but I want to ask you, can you please read my house?" She set down her can of soda. "I haven't found much about the history of the house and the land, and I don't know what Drew's tech can pick up. I bet it'd be faster if you'd take a look."

Tristan pushed his chair back and stood. He towered over her at six feet and two inches tall. Shoving his hands into his pockets, he slumped a little. "I don't know if that's a good idea. What if I pick something up and hurt you?"

"What?" He made no sense. "You just see the past, right?"

"You saw me in this office a few months ago. I don't just see the past, I live it." He walked around his desk. "I'm not an observer. I see the past from someone's point of view. Whoever's energy is strongest, I pick it up. And I channel it. It's weird."

"You figured out your ghost."

"With McKenna's help."

Jaime squared her shoulders. "But McKenna will be there."

"Believe me, McKenna and I have talked about it. I don't think I'm ready." He walked around his desk. "But I'll be there to help."

Tears obscured her vision. All of the fear and worry washed over her. Before she knew it, she was crying in front of her colleague. She stumbled into the nearest chair, embarrassed. She hid her face in her hands. "It didn't look like a ghost this time." She sniffled.

Tristan crouched next to her. "What did it look like?"

"Darkness with red eyes. It hurt my daughter. Put red scratch marks on Ella's arm. If Drew hadn't gotten the door open, I don't know what it might have done to her." She cried harder as the mere idea of Ella dying entered her mind.

Tristan rubbed her back. "Okay. Okay. I'll try. I'll see what I can see."

"Thank you." She threw her arms around him, the relief overwhelming. "Thank you."

Tristan chuckled. "Don't thank me yet. It might be a bust."

"But at least we can try."

Jaime let out a relieved breath. She felt like she had collected all the resources she needed to keep her daughter safe.

The day crawled by. She barely paid attention in her own classes and stumbled through the Western Civilization class she taught. It was not a good day to teach Roman history. She stopped last at the old newspaper archive database on the Blackwood College library website. She searched through a few before she realized it didn't hold any more information about her ghosts.

Bone tired, she peered at her watch. Almost three. Crap! She was going to be late picking up Ella and taking her to Layne's house, their home away from home during the investigation. Her stomach rumbled, reminding her she forgot to eat lunch. Drew and his team would be at her house by six, and she had to let them inside. Maybe they wouldn't mind if she ate dinner while they readied their equipment.

***

A unt Layne!" Ella raced into the waiting hug as soon as she entered the house.

"Ella! My favorite snugglebug!" Layne Williams embraced the girl like she hadn't seen her in a hundred years as opposed to a few days.

Jaime waited with patience for her best friend to release her daughter before she got her chance to hug her. "Thank you for doing this. I know it was short notice."

"No need to thank me. That's what best friends are for." Layne beamed as she led the way into her huge kitchen.

Jaime and Layne had been roommates at the University of North Carolina during their freshmen year. They'd behaved like two eighteen-year-old women who had no clue about the world. Layne tried to talk Jaime out of dating Ella's father, a laid-back guitar player with big blue eyes and long blond hair. Braden Stewart intended to make it big someday and take Jaime on tour with him. That all fell apart when Jaime became pregnant with Ella at the end of her freshman year. Layne, however, did not drop her.

They stayed in touch after Jaime left Carolina and remained close throughout the years. Layne convinced Jaime to go back to school, and then persuaded her to come to

Asheville for both her master's degree and her PhD. She often offered babysitting services.

"Can I go play the drums?" Ella asked, her puppy dog eyes on full display.

Layne laughed loud and long. "They're still in the basement."

"Yes!" She pumped her fist before rushing down the narrow stairs.

"After Mehcad and I get married, I want a dozen just like her," Layne smiled, her dark brown eyes twinkling in the light.

"You might think twice after having the one."

Layne pulled out a bottle of red wine and poured two glasses. She slid Jaime one before taking a sip from her own. Her smooth, brown face grew serious. "Now, what's going on? You sounded terrified on the phone."

Jaime ran her finger around the rim of her glass. "You won't believe me." She studied her friend, a professional, smart businesswoman who relied on facts rather than emotions.

"Try me."

So, Jaime told her about the ghost. How it had asked for help before tearing apart Ella's room. Then she explained about the dark shape that attacked her daughter. Finally, she ended with the ghost hunters who promised to help. Her cheeks burned when she mentioned Drew.

Layne leaned against her island, taking in the whole story. Her expression never betrayed what she was thinking. Her short black curls were perfectly in place as was her tailored suit. Jaime's perfectly put-together friend would never believe her.

She took a casual sip of wine. "Two questions. One, your house has a ghost and a creepy shadow thing?"

"Yes."

"The ghost is some old-timey farm boy who protected Ella from the shadow thing?"

"Yes."

"We're going to need more wine." Layne set her glass on the counter. She retrieved the bottle and refilled Jaime's glass. "Have you been working too hard again?"

Jaime tossed her hands in the air. "I knew you wouldn't believe me."

"I didn't say I didn't believe you, but this is kind of hard to swallow."

"You know me, Layne." Jaime sighed. "When have I ever made up a story like this?" She pressed the tips of her fingers into her chest. "I'm all about facts and proof."

Layne pushed away from the counter and pulled Jaime into a hug. "I know. I know. If you say you saw a ghost, you saw a ghost." She stepped back. "And I did see the scars on Ella's arm. I know for a fact you didn't do that." She cocked her head to the side, studying her friend. "Now, my second question. Is Drew the incredibly attractive man who joined us at the antique shop?"

"Yes." Jaime tried to hide the smile, but her lips curved anyway. She drank some wine to cover it.

"So, this guy you've been seeing is a professional ghost hunter who plans to help you get rid of these ghosts?" Layne gestured with her glass.

Jaime rested her elbows on the hard surface of the counter. "Yeah, I think so. They take this stuff seriously. You remember those three deaths in Hidden Forest Apartments back in August and September? They helped stop it."

Layne's mouth lifted in a tiny smile. "Are you saying a ghost killed those people?"

"I don't know." Jaime shook her head. "But I know they found the decomposed body of a dead girl under the building along with Dr. Smith's body." She tucked a strand of hair behind her ear. "There are so many things we don't know."

Layne shivered. "Yuck."

It all sounded crazy to her own ears, and she saw the ghost with her own two eyes.

Jaime straightened. "I have to go. I have to let the intrepid investigators into my house." She hugged Layne one more time. "I appreciate you looking after Ella."

"Always." Layne squeezed her. "Be careful. Oh, and this Drew guy? He sounds like a keeper. You might want to think about that."

As she pulled into her driveway carrying a bag filled with a burger and fries a while later, she saw Drew sitting on the steps of her front porch. The porch light gave him a halo around his head, bouncing off the blond hair sticking out from underneath his hat. He waved as she sauntered toward him.

"I thought you'd be here later. Did we have a date?" she asked when she reached him.

"No." He turned off the screen on his phone and stuffed it into his jacket pocket. "I wanted to check on you and Ella." He looked around. "Where is Ella? Is she okay?"

His expression of concern touched her heart. "She's fine. Her scratches are scars now. She didn't want to go to school, but I convinced her how cool they were. By the time we got there, she couldn't wait to show them off." She opened the bag of food and pulled out the burger. She held the bag out to him. "Want some fries?"

"I'd love some." Drew reached in and grabbed a handful.

Jaime set to work unwrapping her dinner. "Anyway, she's staying with Layne tonight. Depending on what we find out and how soon you can investigate, I might be staying there myself." She bit into the warm, juicy burger, tomato juice dribbling down her chin. Grabbing a napkin, she wiped the juice off her chin, feeling embarrassed. *Very attractive, Liu,* she thought.

Drew didn't seem to notice. Instead, he popped his handful of fries into his mouth.

Jaime swallowed and started to laugh. "Neither one of us seems to have any table manners, do we? My mom would kill me. And let's not even talk about how my grandmother would react."

Drew chuckled. "They'd be horrified?"

"More like mortified." Jaime took another bite, relishing the taste.

"You've got some mustard here." Drew took a napkin and dabbed the corner of her mouth.

Jaime reached for the napkin and her fingers closed around his warm, rough hand. He had a couple of calluses on his fingertips, hard, comforting spots. She swallowed.

"Thank you." She took the napkin and let go of his hand.

Drew shrugged, pulling back. "No problem."

The rumble of an engine caught Jaime's attention, breaking the quiet moment. She turned to see a green truck and a battered, white van with the Restless Spirits logo written in black on the side park behind Drew's silver Honda Civic in her yard. Her neighbors probably thought she was hosting a party. She finished her burger while Tristan and McKenna stepped out of the truck and Aaron and Tabitha climbed out of the van. They all waved as they walked across the grass.

Jaime held out her bag. "Fries?"

McKenna patted her stomach. "No, but thank you."

Tristan selected a handful and popped it all in like Drew.

Jaime's eyes slid from one to the other. "You two really are best friends."

"I smell fries." Aaron joined them and dipped his hand into the bag as well.

"We just ate," Tabitha said.

"And now I want fries. What's your point?"

Jaime grabbed the railing, hauling herself to her feet. She rolled the bag closed, the crinkling sound filling the night. "Shall we?"

Quiet permeated the house without Ella there. She knew it would only last one night, and Ella had attended sleepovers with her friends before, but Jaime missed her. Her daughter was the light of her life, and the reason ghost hunters and psychics stood in her living room. She set her bag of remaining fries on the kitchen counter before facing Drew and his team. They gathered around the island.

"Where do we start?"

"Well, we tried to find some history on the house and the neighborhood, but I didn't find anything you hadn't already found. You were right, nothing really turned up." McKenna set her pocketbook on the counter next to Jaime's fries.

"Can I ask you for a tour before we start?" Tabitha wandered around the kitchen, studying the cabinets.

"Sure." Jaime turned to Tristan. "Thank you for being here tonight, too."

Tristan sighed. "I can't promise anything, but maybe I can find some answers for you."

"Whatever you need to do, do it. I don't want my daughter attacked again, and we can't afford to move right now." Jaime crossed her arms, feeling more confident about the whole situation. "Okay." She squared her shoulders. "Let's head to the bedroom."

7

A thrill ran through his veins as Drew built the control center in Jaime's living room. A stable fold-out table sat in the middle of the room with a monitor, keyboard, and headphones resting on the center of it. He placed another monitor off to the side. It showed a black and white angle of Ella's room. Black electromagnetic field detectors, walkie-talkies, tape recorders with cassettes, digital recorders, and flashlights covered the rest of the table. He displayed everything in a precise, neat order, unlike the mess in his apartment. Anything the team needed remained available during the whole investigation.

Drew's favorite part of an investigation revolved around gathering the equipment. Sure, it was cool if a real, live ghost appeared, but readying the equipment spoke to his soul. He plugged a wire into a computer, and it sang when he hit the button. He beamed at the sound as it purred like a kitten.

He couldn't count on a ghost putting in an appearance. Nine times out of ten, Drew spent hours in the dark with nothing to show for it. He knew his equipment did its job, whether a ghost showed or not.

Of course, Jaime's haunting seemed more reliable than most so far. He hoped both entities would show up on camera before the investigation ended.

He grunted as he hooked the second monitor to a flat computer case. With all of this equipment, he hoped they could produce answers for Jaime. He hated that she was frustrated. But more than that, he hated that these ghosts targeted her kid. Ella was a great kid.

A hand clapped Drew on the back. "The set up looks great." Aaron leaned down to get a glance at the monitor. "Picture looks good."

"It always does." The cord from the computer slid into the back of the monitor with a satisfying click. Drew straightened and stretched, his back giving way to a satisfying *pop*.

As the computer came on, Aaron dropped into one of the fold-out chairs next to the table. "You know, I've heard everyone else's account of what happened last night except yours. Care to share?"

Drew shrugged, his eyes on the monitor. "Nothing much to tell. Jaime and McKenna told you everything."

Aaron tapped his boot on the hardwood floor. "They said you charged through the door and were ready to take on the big dark spook." He chuckled. "You always like to be the one the ghost beats up."

Drew tapped several keys and another angle of Ella's room appeared. This time, Tabitha stood in front of the closet, waving her arms. She brought her walkie-talkie to her lips.

"I'm ready for my close-up." Her scratchy voice came through the one on the table.

Aaron picked it up. "We hear you and see you loud and clear."

"Awesome!" She bounced a couple of times before walking out of the scene.

"Now, what's bothering you about this case?" Aaron set the walkie-talkie on the edge of the table.

"Nothing's bothering me." Drew zeroed in on fiddling with the nearest digital recorder, making sure it worked and recorded like it should.

"We've worked together long enough for me to tell when something is bothering you. You're frowning, and you never frown." Aaron leaned forward. "I want to make sure all the members of my team have their heads in the game."

"I do." Drew popped open the back of the recorder. Batteries were in their place, right where they should be. "I'm ready, man." He snapped the lid back on and moved on to the next recorder.

"Then I guess you won't mind if I ask McKenna to get a read on you?"

Drew sighed. "Okay. The black shadow thing rattled me." He set the recorder down and turned to Aaron.

"I'm all ears."

"What are we up against? None of us have found any information about that thing. We don't know if it's something separate. We don't know if it's part of the ghost. All we know is it can scratch a scared little girl." Drew grabbed a flashlight and juggled it from one hand to the other. "I don't like walking into something this unprepared." He had admitted his fears out loud for the first time. He didn't like to admit anything.

Everyone thought he had knocked open the door, and he'd tried with all of his strength, but he knew he hadn't done it. The door crashed open on its own. Drew had prepared to face a fully formed ghost. He hadn't expected a big, black shadow taking up half the room, or a bright ghost standing between it and a terrified, exhausted girl. For a split second, before McKenna threw the salt, he had seen the ghost's eyes, and Drew knew in his gut he recognized him.

Something about the shape niggled at his memory. But without proof, he didn't want to bring it up.

Aaron nodded. "I agree."

The flashlight landed in his right hand when Drew stopped juggling it. "Do you? We weren't ready when The White Lady nearly killed McKenna. Or several of those other ghosts we've faced lately. It feels like they're gaining strength, man. How do you know we'll be ready for this?" He slammed the flashlight onto the table, his anger surprising him. Hopping up from the chair, he paced away, restless energy searching for an outlet. He kicked at the leg of his chair before slouching and resting his hands on the back. Drew hadn't even realized how much he worried about this haunting.

Aaron backed up a little, an eyebrow raised. "Whoa, there. Okay. Where is this coming from all of a sudden?"

Drew pulled off his cap and raked a hand through his hair. "That thing up there is scary." He rubbed at his neck. "Maybe I'm not ready to face it again."

Aaron nodded. "All right, then. I'm fine with you manning the control room during the whole investigation. Tristan's here so he can be McKenna's partner."

A soft chuckle escaped Drew. "Oh, yeah. He's the most stable psychic ever."

"He's done pretty well these last couple of months," Aaron said.

Drew had to admit the truth of Aaron's statement. Tristan hadn't been sure he wanted to fully join the team after the whole White Lady thing, but he'd changed his mind. At first, he came to a few meetings and helped McKenna with research. Then he started joining investigations. He had three under his belt, but he only used his psychic power when the team ran out of options. That still didn't mean Drew never worried about his best friend.

"Yeah, he has." Drew straightened and shoved his hat back on his head. "No, I can take a turn on the investigation." He pulled out his ghost disruptor, which still needed a name. He spent the better part of the day tweaking the EMP technology inside, confident he could test it out on an actual ghost. Hopefully, it would stop the ghost, and not all of their equipment. "Besides, it'll be good to give my new toy a test drive."

"Well, if you're up to it." Aaron grunted as he stood.

"I am."

Contrary to what most people believed, investigating ghosts didn't always involve seeing ghosts. For every one ghost Drew saw, he worked on ten investigations where nothing happened. Even though he knew two possible ghosts haunted Jaime's house, had seen the ghost and the shadow with his own eyes, the first hour of this hunt resembled the ten uneventful ones.

Drew manned the first shift at the control center in the bright kitchen with Tristan and McKenna. He trained his eyes on the monitors, searching for anything the investigating team might miss. Since the search was smaller, with one room as the focus, one team of two wandered the area with their equipment. The other three hung back at the control center.

Jaime had left after she gave the team a quick tour. Deep down, Drew wished she had stayed, sitting beside him and helping out. He wanted her around more and more. She brought comfort and fun each hour she spent with him. But in his head, he knew she didn't need to be there.

The walkie-talkie sputtered to life. "A whole lot of nothing is happening," Aaron reported.

"I see that." The chair squeaked as Drew leaned back in it. His rear end hurt from sitting on the hard surface for so long.

"We're going to give it some more time, then the psychics are in charge. Be ready, Tristan."

Tristan grabbed the walkie-talkie. "Yeah, yeah."

"You're going to be fine." McKenna rubbed his back.

Tristan stretched and yawned. "This is the glamorous life." He blinked at his watch. "And it's only eight-thirty. I feel the time flying by." His tone dripped with sarcasm as one corner of his mouth quirked.

"It pays the bills." Drew picked up the ghost disruptor and flipped open the side. "Seriously, though, how do you feel?" He tapped his temple. "I know this is your first time in Jaime's house."

It wasn't that long ago that Tristan feared his power. Drew watched him struggle with it, and he hated that he couldn't help him. Thanks to McKenna, Tristan reacted with more command. His control still wasn't perfect, but he at least tried. For a long while, Tristan cut himself off from everyone and everything and hid in his parent's house. It took a lot of coaxing from Drew and Zack, their college friend, to get him out into the world again. Sadly, Zack's death had forced Tristan to trust in his power again.

Drew grew up watching Tristan see snippets of the past. Sometimes they were quick flashes, but most of the time, they were deep dives. If a vision swept Tristan away, his whole personality changed. Before McKenna came along, Drew held on for dear life, suffering a few kicks and punches to bring his friend back to himself. However, McKenna acted as the best grounding force for Tristan. She helped steady him and calm him when things got out of hand. Drew didn't know if her empathic ability helped or if Tristan simply loved her, but she brought Tristan back to himself every time.

"I'm good." Tristan crossed his arms. "She was right. Her house is newer so not a lot of history is knocking at the door." He looked around the room. "Although, it's a good thing I don't read objects. I think all of her furniture is older than all of us put together."

"I asked her about them, and she said most of the objects have been with her since the beginning," McKenna said. "The only thing new is the fiddle over the couch."

"You know, I didn't even think about that, and I should have." Drew paused from tightening some of the wires inside of his machine. Setting the gun-shaped disruptor on the table, he stood. His chair scraped against the hardwood floor. He walked around the kitchen and into the dining room where he had a clear view of the fiddle. He thought it strange that its vibe infected him with this weird feeling. He rested a hand on his stomach as it did a somersault.

"Is this the fiddle in question?" Tristan joined him in the dining room, McKenna with him.

"Yeah, that's it. I did see a shadow around it, but I thought it was my imagination." Drew crossed his arms. "After all, if the haunting is coming from it, why did both the ghost and that black smoke show up in Ella's room? It's upstairs on the opposite end of the house."

"Maybe her ability attracted both?" McKenna suggested.

Tristan regarded it for a long moment. A change came into his eyes, and he ambled toward the fiddle.

"Tristan?" McKenna followed him.

Dread settled in Drew's chest like a rock. After all this time in the house, did something get past Tristan's defenses? Or did his friend let something in? Tristan didn't read objects so why the sudden change?

His best friend cocked his head to the right, like a dog

trying to understand something. Tristan blinked. "Do you hear music?"

"What music are you hearing?" McKenna rested a hand on his shoulder.

"A quick reel." Tristan's brow furrowed as he reached out, like he was trying to capture the music.

"A reel? What's that?" Drew asked.

Tristan snapped like he searched for the right words. "It's fast fiddle music. Kind of like country or bluegrass, but quicker. Like Irish music." His green eyes lost focus as he drifted closer to the antique fiddle on the wall.

Drew exchanged a glance with McKenna. He ran back into the kitchen and collected his disruptor, an EMF detector, and his phone. Keeping the detector in his hand, he stuffed the disruptor into his back pocket, handle out. He found Tristan and McKenna standing in front of the couch staring at the fiddle as if they studied a painting. He held out his phone and pressed record. He hadn't placed a camera in front of the fiddle, but he needed to record the moment.

Lately, Tristan controlled his power better. He rarely got a vision he didn't prepare for. But sometimes, especially when a ghost became involved, the past pushed its way through Tristan's constructed mental walls.

Tristan inched toward the couch. His face changed, taking on a bored expression. "It's going to take forever to build this house." His accent changed, more musical, the r's harder and clipped. "We're behind schedule already."

"What house are we building?" Drew watched his friend through his phone, unmoving.

"It'll be big enough for you and our family." Tristan lifted his hand and touched the fiddle on the wall. "I can't wait to teach the baby how to play. Music will fill this house."

The lights on top of the EMF detector lit. First one, then two, until all five brightened. The air grew colder, and the fiddle gave off a soft glow. Drew nodded to McKenna. She clicked off the overhead light. He saw the object as if the light never went off. It beamed in a glimmer of its own. He framed it in the shot.

"I'm going to love you forever." Tristan's voice had taken on a soft Irish brogue, deeper than his own voice.

"Tristan, step back. What do you see?" McKenna curled her fingers around Tristan's hands. She turned him away from the fiddle. "Tell me what's going on."

"Tristan?" Drew wanted to shake his friend awake and pull him out of the vision. But he knew Tristan needed to see it through. "What do you see, man?" He edged closer to the fiddle. The glow brightened, almost as if it welcomed him. He felt a strange pull in his blood. The same pull he felt in the antique store and the first night Jaime had seen the ghost. The night Drew witnessed the dark, icy shadow.

"When I get your da's permission, we're going to settle here and visit Ireland. Just you and me." In the radiance, Drew saw Tristan press a hand to McKenna's stomach, palm flat, his fingers spread. "And the little one."

"Tristan, separate yourself. What are you seeing?" McKenna continued to try and get through to him as she lifted his hand away from her. "Who are you? Who's pregnant?"

The metal on the detector warmed in Drew's hand. It got so hot he dropped it. It clattered onto the hardwood floor. He gripped his phone, not wanting to lose it the same way. He wasn't losing a moment of footage.

The fiddle continued to beam, calling to him. It was ridiculous. Drew possessed no psychic ability, nor did he know how to play a fiddle, or any musical instrument for that matter. But it seemed familiar, welcoming. Propping his phone on the side table with it still recording, he risked walking past Tristan and McKenna and closing his fingers around the neck. Even though the air was freezing, the fiddle was balmy to the touch.

Drew hefted it off the wall, his fingers aching to play it.

"No! Don't!" Tristan jerked away from McKenna, his eyes wide open, but unseeing. He held out his hands in front of him as if trying to stop something only he could see.

"Tristan, please," McKenna begged. "Control it."

The light twisted and curled off the fiddle. It formed a shape in the middle of the room, right in front of Drew, creating the figure of a man. Drew saw right through him, but he made out blue overalls and a brown wide-brimmed hat with short blond hair peeking out underneath. It was the ghost who protected Ella the night before. But the ghost's eyes stopped his heart. This time, he stood close enough to see them clearly. His grandfather's eyes. His father's eyes. His own eyes. The Keane hazel eyes. It chilled him to the bone.

"Help me." The ghost's voice crackled in Drew's ears, his Irish brogue matching Tristan's. "Please find my treasure."

Tristan screamed. Drew glanced away from the ghost to see his friend fall back, a hand clutching his chest. McKenna went down with him.

The dark pressed against Drew, as if a weight settled over him. He tried to breathe but couldn't. The fiddle fell from his fingers and landed on the couch. The ghost vanished. The darkness tightened around him, and he coughed. Air! He needed air! Where was the door? The light? Why couldn't he breathe?

Feet pounded down the stairs. Tabitha's voice sounded a million miles away.

"Drew! Tristan! McKenna! We heard a scream. What's going on?"

Drew opened his mouth to answer her, but no sound came out. He was frozen in place, unable the move. The darkness closed in, obscuring the living room. He dropped to his knees. Sharp ice prickled his skin from all directions. This was it. This was the end. A sinister voice whispered in his ear. It held no Irish accent this time, but it possessed the rhythm of the Blue Ridge Mountains.

"Give up, boy. Give in. You're mine." It snaked around him, wrapping him as tightly as the darkness. "Give in to me. I knew I'd find you, and you'll die like the rest."

8

N o." It eked out as a whisper. For a second, Drew thought he made no sound until he noticed the word pushing past his lips. He shoved at the shadow. "No." Louder this time. "No!"

He worked to move his arm, sweating with the effort. His hand wrapped around the handle of the disruptor in his back pocket. He yanked it out, flipped the switch, and wading through the thick smoke enveloping him, pointed it into the darkness. With a steady whir, it charged. Drew pressed the trigger. The black mist burst apart, dissolving into tiny pieces. Then everything electric in the immediate area died.

"What the hell?" Aaron dropped to his knees and eased the disruptor out of Drew's cramped fingers. Small puffs of white smoke plumed out of the back of the gun-shaped machine. Aaron swore, almost dropping it. "This thing is hot!"

Drew gulped in one breath, then another. Sweet, sweet air. The heater cranked on with a moan, and the overhead light flooded the room.

Tristan lay on his back, his eyes closed. But his chest rose and fell. McKenna and Tabitha sat next to him. Drew crawled over to shake his friend's shoulder. Tristan moaned. Drew shook harder. His friend's eyes popped open.

Tristan's hand shot up as his eyes squinted. "Someone dim the lights." His voice held its normal cadence.

Drew breathed a sigh of relief. "Thank God."

Aaron held out a hand, assisting Drew to his feet. Tabitha and McKenna pulled Tristan off the floor.

"What happened?" Aaron demanded, fury on his face.

Tristan ran a hand over his chest. "I think I was shot."

"I thought you were dead." Drew rested his hands on his knees as he tried to catch his breath. "I thought I was going to die." He took one breath, then another, trying to get his heart rate back to a normal rhythm. The tension in his muscles lessened as the adrenaline disappeared. He ached from head to toe.

"Drew, you're sick with fear." McKenna rubbed his back.

"I think I know where the ghost is coming from and what that dark shadow wants." He straightened and met McKenna's eyes. "The darkness wants me."

Minutes later, he sat at the kitchen table, a water bottle in his trembling hands. Cool and comforting water slid down Drew's throat. He couldn't get enough of it. He chugged the whole bottle, the plastic crinkling as it emptied. He gripped it like a lifeline. No one said a word until he set it down on the fold-out table in the command center with a thump.

Aaron sprawled in the chair next to him, his legs spread and his arms crossed. He lifted a brow. "What did you mean when you said the shadow wanted you?"

"I don't know." Why did he still quake in his shoes? His hand trembled as he pulled his hat off his head. "He...It... wanted me to give up, to go ahead and die." He remembered the deep and menacing voice rumbling in his ear. But was it real, or all in his head?

"Why does he want you dead?" Tabitha asked. She perched on the edge of the table, her camera next to her.

"I don't know!" Everyone jumped at his shout. He raised a hand while he rubbed his aching head with the other. "I'm sorry. Still a little shaken up."

"And you thought the ghost had the same eyes as you?" McKenna studied him with worry in her eyes. She and Tristan sat on the other side of the table, nothing blocking her view. They boxed away most of the equipment, leaving the smooth surface clear.

"Same color and everything." Drew scratched his forehead with his thumb. "He was as close to me as I am to you. This ghost wasn't like The White Lady. He was transparent, but in full color. Jaime wasn't exaggerating." He reached for another bottle of water. His mouth tasted dry like a desert. No amount of liquid seemed to take it away. He twisted off the cap and drank half the bottle in one gulp. "Tristan, what about you?" Drew gestured with the bottle. "I thought you were dead for a minute. What the hell did you see?"

Tristan rubbed his chest. "You weren't the only one who thought I was dead. It still hurts." He sighed. "The first thing I saw was a lot of people building a house. The man I was knew them as friends and neighbors. Mountains surrounded the valley, and everyone was laughing and talking.

"A pregnant woman wearing a white shirtwaist and a long, brown skirt wrapped her arms around me." He blinked. "Him. Her red hair was pulled into a bun, kind of like they did in the early 1900's. I...he reached out and rubbed her belly." His brow wrinkled in concentration. "He loved her, but he was scared for her. For her and their child."

"He was building a house, but he wanted to take her back to Ireland?" McKenna asked.

"Yeah, for a visit." Tristan pushed his curls back as he blew out a breath. "He came from Ireland, fresh off the boat, I think." He nodded to the instrument lying on the dining room table. "He wanted to show her where he came from and maybe see the rest of the world. But he wanted a place to call home, too."

"And the fiddle?" Drew asked. He soaked in the details of the story Tristan told.

"It was his. I saw him play it."

"But who was he? The ghost or the shadow?" Aaron asked. The heavy thump of his footsteps moved back and forth behind Drew's chair. Sometime during the conversation, he jumped from his chair and paced. The agitated action worsened Drew's headache, but he didn't have the energy to tell his boss to stop.

"Definitely the ghost. The accent matched," Drew confirmed. He noticed his best friend sensed the ghost before it arrived. He couldn't read objects, but he read the dead's energy as if they were still alive.

"Did you get his name? Her name? The place? Anything?" Tabitha pressed.

"No." Tristan groaned, leaning back in the chair. "I wasn't prepared and didn't pay attention. I'm sorry."

"It's okay. You weren't ready." McKenna rubbed his back and rested her head on his shoulder.

Tristan grimaced. "I should've been, from the moment I walked into this house."

Drew met his friend's eyes. "What about when you clutched your chest. What happened then?"

Tristan shrugged. "I don't know. All I know is the scene changed, and I was staring down the barrel of a shotgun. It fired, and everything went black. I didn't even see who pulled the trigger."

Drew polished off the water. He crinkled the second empty bottle, setting it next to the first. "All the activity centers around that fiddle." The strange pull continued to call him, even with the instrument in a separate room. From the kitchen, he glanced at the fiddle laying on the dining room.

Drew insisted on setting it there, where he could keep an eye on it. It no longer glowed. Instead, it was a simple, old, orange fiddle with missing strings and dents and dings all over it, like it had been in the shop when he and Jaime found it. He saw nothing weird or frightening about it.

"I don't want to jump to conclusions until we review the footage and the tapes." Aaron stretched and yawned. "McKenna, let Jaime know we're getting ready to pack up. I'd like to ask her a few questions about this fiddle before we leave."

McKenna waved her phone. "Already done."

Drew lost track of how long he sat in his chair, his arms resting on the table. He felt steadier, no longer shaking, and his nerves calmed down. His stomach had stopped flipping as well. Everyone around him gathered equipment, wrapped cords, boxed monitors, and collected the cameras from Ella's room. But Drew stayed in his spot, not ready to move.

He regarded the old instrument. How old was it? Who did it belong to? Why did it have such an effect on him? And was it the key to the hauntings? He shifted out of his seat and headed into the dining room. Not realizing he had moved closer to it, he touched one of the strings. A tiny spark of electricity shot through his hand, and he yanked it back.

Out of nowhere, a faint voice said, "Help me."

Drew jumped and scurried away from the table. Now he wanted to put as much distance between himself and the fiddle. But the urge to touch it ran through his system, which was the weirdest thing of all. Until that point, he had held no desire to play a fiddle, but the pull was so strong.

The kitchen door swung open, and Jaime walked in. The

heaviness in the room lifted. All of a sudden, it seemed like Drew could breathe again.

Jaime stiffened when McKenna texted her. Drew's team explained that they planned to end the investigation around midnight. The clock on her phone displayed ten o'clock. Had the ghost already shown himself? She raced into her kitchen through the back door, dying to know what Drew had found. Even better, maybe the ghost and the shadow left for good. She prepared to return to her normal life.

She smiled at Drew. "All done?"

"Yeah." He delivered a tight, close-lipped smile that didn't reach his eyes. It looked odd on his face. "Met the ghost and the shadow-smoke thing, too."

Oh, no! Her heart thudded in her chest. "Are you okay?" She checked him over, searching for bruises, cuts, or worse injuries. If the apparitions in her house hurt him, she'd never forgive herself.

Drew put his hat back on his head. "I will be." He didn't sound sure. His tone didn't contain his usual bravado and dull weariness replaced it. Jaime didn't like this version of Drew. She felt like she spoke to a stranger.

Aaron sauntered into the room and set the camera case he carried next to the wall. He held a hand out to Jaime. "Thank you for letting us come in here. We tried not to disturb anything."

Jaime tore her gaze from Drew and shook his outstretched hand. "Thank you for investigating. McKenna said you had a few questions for me?"

"Yeah. I wanted to ask you about this fiddle. Where did you get it?"

Jaime looked at the fiddle. "Drew could answer that. We found it at an antique shop. What does the fiddle have to do with anything?" She frowned as she looked back at Aaron.

"I think the ghost, and maybe the shadow, is attached to it," Drew answered before Aaron could. "I saw it glow."

Jaime opened her mouth slightly, closed it, and then opened again. She tried to sort out what Drew said. "It glowed?" She leaned closer to the instrument. "I never saw it do that, and I don't think Ella did, either." She straightened. "You really saw it glow?"

Drew nodded.

"But Ella only ever saw the ghost and the shadow in her room. How can it be attached to the fiddle?" *Not the fiddle. Please not the fiddle.* She loved that ridiculous instrument.

Aaron hooked a thumb in the pocket of his jeans. "Sometimes an object rather than a place, is haunted. Based on what Drew said, I think that's the case. But I also think Ella's psychic energy attracted both entities. Does Ella spend most of her time in her room?"

"Yeah. She's almost a teenager." Jaime examined the fiddle again. She didn't notice anything different about it.

Aaron picked up the camera case. "Her power might have called them. One to ask for help, and the other to stop her."

She shoved the instrument away. "Then get the fiddle out of here. I want that thing as far away from my daughter as possible." Jaime felt like she swallowed a lead ball. The fiddle was no longer her favorite antique. It could leave her house at any time.

"Can we take it back to the office with us? Just to see if I'm right." Drew rubbed the back of his neck.

"Sure." Jaime tucked a strand of hair behind her ear. "If it's the source of all the trouble, I don't want it back." She cast another glance at it, her stomach queasy. To think, such a small thing caused so much trouble. "I'll find something else to put over the couch." It looked so perfect hanging in that spot, but Ella's wellbeing was more important.

"Good idea. We still have footage and recordings to review before we can share our all of our findings." Aaron tightened his grip on the case.

Jaime nodded. "I understand."

Aaron hauled the case out of the house. Tabitha followed him out with an armload full of electronics. McKenna and Tristan stayed outside loading the van. They left Drew and Jaime alone in the house.

"Are you really okay?" Jaime leaned down and hugged him. She pressed a light kiss to his shoulder. "Tell me what happened."

Drew sighed and then spilled out how Tristan saw a vision of a young couple in the mountains and the ghost appeared out of the fiddle. She let go of him as she sank into the chair next to him. He continued, explaining how he thought the ghost's eyes matched his own. He then told her about the shadow wanting him dead and almost succeeding in killing him.

Drew took a breath. "I'm doing better. More shaken up than anything." This time the smile that slid across his face reached his eyes. He appeared more like himself. "The shadow didn't scratch me." This was the Drew that Jaime knew.

"Well, that's a relief." She chuckled, her worry easing. She crossed to her dining room table, studying the fiddle. How could one small instrument cause so much trouble? Or how could a person's soul be attached to it? "Do you think you and the ghost are related?" she asked as she reached out to touch the fiddle.

"Yeah, but I don't know him. I don't think I've ever seen a picture of him."

The moment her fingers connected with the strings, electricity zinged along her arm. She jerked her hand back in surprise more than pain. "I think the fiddle shocked me."

"Really?" Drew leaned forward. "It shocked me, too."

"Static electricity?"

Aaron ducked back into the room. "Ready for us to take it?"

Jaime nodded, still a little sad to see the piece go.

Aaron retrieved the fiddle, tucking it under his arm. As he strode away, Jaime noted no sparks when the other man touched it. She filed away the weird event as she watched it go.

Drew scratched his head under his hat. "I don't think static electricity shocks like that," he said when he and Jaime were alone again. He stood behind her and rubbed her arms. "I thought it shocked me because I might be related, but why would it shock you?" She turned to face him. "Has it ever done that before?"

"No." Each revelation grew stranger by the minute.

"Well, with it out of the house, I think Ella might be safe. Like Aaron said, I want to review all the data we collected, but my gut tells me all the trouble begins and ends with that fiddle." He moved his hat back and pressed his forehead against hers.

Jaime closed her eyes. His presence made the rest of the world melt away, leaving only the two of them. It had been a long time since Jaime dated the same man for almost two months, and she didn't remember any others making her feel this safe and steady. She opened her eyes, looking into his hazel ones.

"Thank you for protecting Ella, but will you be safe? If whatever's in that fiddle wants you dead, you need to stay away from it."

Drew stepped back, the small distance already cold. "We'll

take safety measures. Put salt around it and keep it away from my office. I'll be careful."

Jaime bit her lip, a thought occurring to her. "You said you have to find out what the ghost wants before it'll leave, right? How are you going to find his treasure?"

"I don't know." Drew shrugged. He turned the folding table on its side and closed one set of legs. "After we review everything, we'll try to find out who he is and what that shadow thing is." He shifted the table in the other direction, locking the other set of legs in place.

"So, now what?" Jaime peered into his hazel eyes.

"I think I owe you a date." Leaning the table against the wall, Drew closed the distance between them. He took her face in his hands, pressing his lips to hers. Her whole body tingled as she kissed him back. All thoughts of ghosts and shadows left her head as she was swept away.

9

Jaime tossed and turned on Layne's hard, lumpy pull-out couch. The springs squeaked every time she moved. Even though she knew she and Ella were safe there, she couldn't squash the worry. Drew said he believed the ghost and the shadow remained tied to the fiddle, and Aaron had taken the fiddle away from the house. But what if he made a mistake? What if they were attached to something else in her house? And even worse, Drew said that the shadow wanted him dead.

She remembered how icy the black smoke was and how red its eyes were. It didn't have much of a shape, just deep darkness. It brought to mind stories about *yaoguai* that her grandmother used to tell her—demons who tricked and killed to gain immortality. Was there any truth to those stories? She used to think crazy people believed in those things, even when her mother told her not to be so foolish.

"There is so much in this world we don't know about," her mother often said. "How can you be so sure these things don't exist? After all, I always know things before they happen."

But if it was a demon, how could she fight it? Did anyone at Restless Spirits know how? Maybe she was wildly speculating and overreacting.

She groaned. She didn't know enough to form an answer.

So she changed her thoughts to happier matters, like the kiss. She had kissed Drew a few times during the last couple of months, but the last kiss ranked at the top. Her whole body warmed as she remembered the feel of his lips, the light prickle of the stubble on his jaw, and the tight, comforting way he held her.

She smiled as she snuggled deeper into her blanket. She thought more and more about him as the months went on. The longer he stayed around, the more attached she'd become. And if Ella became attached along with her, the inevitable breakup would be more devastating. She convinced herself the end was coming, and the ghosts would probably hasten it along. Nobody wanted to take on a ready-made family. She dated enough guys and heard that excuse enough times to know. But she wanted this relationship to last. *Please don't let it end too soon.*

"Mom?" Ella stood at the bottom of the stairs. Jaime tried to see her features in the soft glimmer of the streetlight outside.

"Ella, what are you doing up?"

The girl shrugged her small shoulders. "I woke up." She crossed the room and crawled into the bed with her mother. "Can I sleep with you?"

"Of course." Jaime moved over as Ella settled next to her. She cuddled as close to Jaime as possible. Jaime covered her daughter with her arm and stroked her hair, like she used to do when Ella was younger.

"Did the ghost show up for the ghost hunters?" Ella's voice sounded small, not like the cocky preteen she pretended to be.

"He did."

"And the black smoke?" Ella huddled closer.

Jaime considered lying to her, but that wouldn't be fair. "Yes."

"Did they make them go away?"

Jaime sighed. "I hope so." She told Ella about the fiddle and how Drew thought both hauntings came from it. "Since it's not in our house anymore, we may not see the ghosts again."

Quiet descended on the room, and Jaime thought Ella slept. She twisted on her side, ready to do the same.

Ella's voice broke the silence. "The ghost didn't want to hurt me. I know that now. He tried to protect me from the smoke."

"I think you're right." Jaime looked at the low streetlight out the window. The neighborhood stayed silent at this time of night.

"Mom, do you think if I actually did find his treasure, he wouldn't haunt people anymore?" Ella's voice held a thoughtfulness to it.

Jaime rolled back to her, making out her small form in the dark. She lay face up, looking at the ceiling. "I don't know, baby."

"If the ghost hunters need to do that, can I help?"

Jaime raised up on her arm. "Do you really want to do that?"

"Yeah." Ella sat up and drew her knees to her chest. "I kind of feel bad for him. And he did help save me from the smoke."

Jaime smoothed down her daughter's hair. Her heart pumped faster as she thought of Ella wanting to help a wayward ghost, especially if it put her in harm's way. "We'll see. We can talk about this if it comes up, okay?"

"Okay." Ella threw herself into her mother's arms. Jaime hugged her tightly to her chest.

"The ghost hunters are going to help the ghost, right?"

"I don't know, baby. I hope so."

Minutes later, both mother and daughter drifted off to sleep.

———

*J*aime *woke to find herself in the middle of a dark forest. A touch of light trickled in through the trees, enough to see by. The woods smelled earthy, damp, and strong. She pushed herself upright, brushing sticks and dirt from her pants. Leaves crunched under her feet as she walked through the underbrush. She wrapped her arms around herself, but the air didn't feel cold. In fact, it felt more like spring.*

Her intuition told her to walk forward, so she did. She curved around trees, searching for a path. But one didn't appear. As she walked around another tree, a soft song filtered through the vast, quiet place. She stopped and listened, but she was too far away to identify the tune.

She moved toward it, the lyrics becoming clearer with each passing step. She still didn't recognize the song, but it sounded like a lullaby.

"Down in the valley, valley so low. Hang your head over, hear the wind blow."

A lady's voice sang it, slow and mournful. Each note perfect and on pitch. She had a Southern twang, the music of the mountains. Jaime heard the same accent in Drew's voice, only his came across lighter.

Jaime stepped into a clearing and stopped. A woman wearing a blue shirt waist and a long, dark blue skirt sat in a patch of sunlight, rocking a wooden cradle. Her red hair was unbound and streaming down her back to reach her waist. Her voice rang out clear through the forest. She lifted her head and smiled.

"I've been waiting for you," she said as she continued to rock the cradle. It creaked with each pass.

Jaime glanced behind her, confused. "Excuse me?"

"Yes, you." The woman nodded. "You can come over and sit a spell. The baby just fell asleep, but he won't pay us any mind." The woman sat in a wooden rocking chair. She gestured to a similar chair next to her that Jaime swore wasn't there a moment ago.

"Where am I?" Jaime asked as she crossed to the woman and took the offered seat. She ran her hand over smooth light brown wood. It groaned as she settled in.

"A safe place. It's the only place in the whole forest where he can't reach us." The woman looked fondly at her baby in the crib. "You have a little one, too, don't you?"

"I do. She's not so little anymore." Jaime peered into the crib. The baby moved in its sleep, its eyes closed and its breathing even.

"They're always little to us." The woman studied Jaime with clear blue eyes. "You're quite a bit prettier than I thought you'd be. He chose well."

"Who is he?" The conversation grew stranger by the minute. She felt like she'd been dropped into Wonderland where nothing made sense.

"You know who he is." The woman placed a cool hand on Jaime's. "And he needs your help. He can't do this alone. The danger'll be coming for him."

"Who? Do what alone?" Jaime took in the dark forest surrounding them. "Where are we?"

"I expect I'll be seeing you again. Keep your eyes and ears open, Jaime Liu. We're all going to need you. You and your girl." The woman nodded. "We've been waiting for you for a long time."

A roar rumbled in the trees beyond the circle of light. Jaime started, fear creeping through her heart. She saw matching fear in the woman's eyes. "Get on home to your girl. He knows I found you. Listen and learn, and keep him safe."

Jaime sat straight up, the lumpy couch mattress creaking underneath her. Light from the streetlamp illuminated the room. Next to her, Ella snored. She crawled over to the side table and picked up her phone. Almost five in the morning. She set the phone back on the table, lying back down. She had a dream, a strange dream that came from all the bits and pieces of everything that had happened over the past few days. That was all.

But if it was a dream, why did it feel so real? Jaime swore she still smelled wood and earth. And why could she remember everything the strange woman said?

Drew woke the next morning with the memory of Jaime in his arms and her lips on his. He lay in bed long after his alarm beeped, thinking about every detail of her. He needed her after facing the black smoke ghost. With a groan, he rose and ran his fingers through his messy hair. As much as he wanted to spend the whole day thinking about Jaime, he had a possible family ghost to research.

Since he didn't have to be at work until that afternoon, Drew made his way to the public library. Settling at a computer with a bit of privacy, he dove into the research databases and found the link to an ancestry website. *McKenna and Tristan aren't the only ones who know how to research,* he smirked. His fingers poised over the keyboard, ready to type in his grandfather's name when he heard her voice behind him.

"Drew?" Jaime slid into the empty chair next to him. "I thought you'd still be asleep."

"I thought about it." The whole day turned brighter. "What are you doing here?"

"Well." Her cheeks flushed a bright pink. "I was in the mood to do a little research on the fiddle."

"But you don't have to worry about it anymore. I've got this."

"I know, but I had the strangest dream last night. When I woke up, I couldn't stop thinking about it. Ella is at school, and all my classes are later today, and I thought, why not go to the library?" She pulled a notebook and a pen out of her bag and settled at the station next to him. "What are you doing here?"

He gestured to the computer. "Looking up my family tree."

Her light brown eyes widened and pure joy spread across her features. "Can I look with you?" She moved her chair closer. Drew caught a whiff of lemon and a light floral scent he couldn't identify. He wanted to bury his face in her hair, but that would be weird in a public place.

"You know, Tristan is the only person I ever knew who got that excited about history." He leaned back in the chair. "How did you get into history?"

Jaime propped her chin in her hand. "Well, I kind of fell into it, really. My grandmother used to tell me stories about being a kid in China and the trip to America. She was young when her family immigrated here. I always loved listening to those family stories. It's my connection with her. Still is since she's very much alive and living it up traveling the world with my grandfather.

"Anyway, my parents were hoping I'd go the doctor route or work in the tech industry like my brother Alan does. But I did none of those things. I want to find a way to bring the past alive. I want to share those stories like my nai nai shared them. So, I teach history."

Drew nodded. "But why get your PhD? You could teach high school."

Jaime laughed, a big, loud, wonderful laugh. The older woman sitting across from them leaned to the left and shushed them. Jaime covered her mouth. "Sorry." She turned back to Drew, and he noticed she pitched her voice lower. "I actually tried that a couple of years ago. I am not cut out for that age group. Teens are still a little too young and have no interest in what I'm trying to teach."

"So, you'd rather teach adults?"

"Definitely. Once I get my PhD, I'll finally become that doctor my parents always wanted. And, hopefully, get a job at one of the colleges around here."

Drew raised his eyebrows. "Sounds like a solid plan."

"Thank you. I just hope it's a job with more teaching and less publishing. That part scares the crap out of me. I'm the world's worst writer." She tossed her hair over her shoulder. "I'd rather talk about history instead of write about it." She tapped the monitor. "And speaking of history, let's see what secrets the Keane family tree holds."

Drew sighed. She was right. He typed in his grandfather's name and birthdate and waited to see what hits appeared. Many people shared the name Henry Keane, but only one seemed to be born near Boone in 1940. Drew clicked on the link. A family tree filled the screen.

"It can't be that easy," he mumbled.

"Sometimes you stumble on things," Jaime said. "Plus, a lot of people love to fill these genealogy sites."

Someone listed his grandfather as an uncle, which meant the tree belonged to a distant cousin. He scrolled up to see his great-grandparents' names, Thomas and Sarah Keane. He followed above Thomas's name and the hunt came to a dead stop. For Thomas's father, it listed only Keane, but his mother had the name Melinda Beauchamp.

"I knew it wouldn't be easy." Drew fell back in the chair, hope dissipating.

Jaime leaned forward. "Melinda's name is a link." She clicked on it. Another family tree appeared, but this one had pictures. Jaime gasped. "That's her."

"That's who?" Drew straightened and cocked his head.

"That's the woman from my dream."

Drew took a minute to process this information. "You mean to tell me you dreamed about my great-great grandmother?"

Jaime leaned away. "I didn't know she was your great-great grandmother at the time. She didn't even tell me her name."

Drew didn't realize they raised their voices until the same older woman interrupted them with a glare. "Do you mind? Some of us are trying to work here." She went back to her computer with a huff.

"Come on, let's walk. I'll buy you something to eat, and you can tell me about that dream." Drew closed the site and logged off the computer. He slid his chair back. Curiosity buzzed inside him.

Jaime gathered her things. "You're on."

Jaime bundled into her thick coat tight to fight off the chilly morning as she and Drew left the library. They headed down the sidewalk, the crisp, smoky scent of autumn hanging in the air. A few people strolled down the hill past the shops and restaurants, but not as many as on the weekends. Most of them were tourists, in town to drive through the mountains and enjoy the changing leaves. Autumn was peak tourist season in the mountains, and Asheville welcomed them all.

Jaime enjoyed the fact she didn't have to keep her voice down anymore. She knew that lady wanted to punch both of them. She had pinched her face and pursed her lips after returning to her screen.

Drew adjusted the brim of his cap before stuffing his hands into his coat pockets. "Now, tell me about the dream."

As they walked down the hill from the library, Jaime described everything she remembered from the dream. She told him about the woods and the clearing. How Melinda sounded, the words she said. "She was younger than she appeared in the picture. Possibly in her twenties."

"And you're sure it was my great-great grandmother?" Drew peered down at her.

Jaime shrugged. "I don't have any proof, but she resembled the woman in the picture." She rubbed her hands together, trying to get heat into them. "If it was your great-great grandmother, how could I be dreaming about her? I never saw her before. Plus, I'm not psychic."

They rounded the curve, heading for a small restaurant tucked away on a side street. Jaime breathed a sigh of relief when they stepped inside and the heat greeted them. Glorious, glorious heat. The hostess greeted them and showed them to a table in the back corner. Nice and private.

Drew shrugged out of his coat. "Are you sure it wasn't a reaction to everything that's happened this past week?"

"I'm not." Jaime leaned over her menu. "But how did I know what your great-great grandmother looked like?"

"Good question." Drew scratched the stubble on his chin.

A plucky waitress with rainbow-colored hair appeared and took their orders. With a smile and a nod, she disappeared again.

Drew stretched out on his side of the dark booth. "Tell me again what she said."

"She said she'd been waiting for me, and that he chose well. Whoever he is. She didn't elaborate on that part." Jaime sighed as she raked her fingers through her hair. Even though it all seemed so normal in the dream, it sounded crazy to her ears in the daylight. She thought Drew believed her. He didn't laugh, at least. But she couldn't be sure. What if she was losing her mind? "She then said she needed me. My girl and me."

"Was there anything else?" Drew asked.

"Only that he needs me, and I have to keep him safe. Next, something in the woods roared, and I woke up." The waitress set a Mountain Dew in front of Jaime. She thanked her before taking a sip. The sweet, fizzy taste grounded her. "I still don't know who this *he* is."

"Well." Drew sipped his coffee. "If it is my great-great grandmother, and it's tied to all of this craziness, maybe she meant the ghost in the hat and the overalls?"

"The one who might be related to you? The one who might be the Keane she married?"

"Exactly."

Jaime lifted a brow. "How am I supposed to protect him? He's dead."

Drew opened his mouth for a moment before closing it a second later. "I don't know," he admitted.

Protecting a ghost. The thought slid around in her brain. *Protect him from what? The shadow?* If he needed shielding from the shadow, why did he block the shadow from Ella? She twirled a lock of her hair as she ruminated on it.

"I think I'm missing something," she said.

The food arrived at that moment, stopping Drew from answering. Plates of eggs, bacon, sausage, and Jaime's blueberry waffles filled every spot on the table. Drew's eyes widened with delight as he picked up his fork and dug in. "Breakfast. Best meal of the day."

A smile tugged at the corners of Jaime's mouth. She caught Drew's delight and let it lift her mood. Between his fight with the shadow thing and her strange dream, they had both spent a rough night. Sitting and having breakfast with Drew made everything wonderful and normal again.

She covered her waffle in whipped cream. Satisfied at that she had covered every last inch, she took her first bite. Light, fluffy heaven danced on her tongue. Every bit of it.

Jaime pointed her fork at Drew. "Do you realize that we're finally having that date you promised me?"

Drew appeared thoughtful. "You're right. Why didn't I think of breakfast originally?"

"Yeah, why didn't you?" Jaime took another bite, a smile tugging at the corners of her mouth. "So, I have to know." She sipped some Mountain Dew, the sweet caffeinated nectar of the gods. "Why ghost hunting?"

"Why ghost hunting?" Drew echoed as he bit into a piece of bacon.

"Yeah, you asked me about history earlier, so why ghost hunting?"

"I think you mean paranormal investigating. It's my vocation, remember?" Drew chuckled as Jaime tossed a napkin at him. "Okay. The first time I saw a ghost, I was about five or six. I spent the night with Papa B, and I saw the ghost of a man. He walked through the living room wall and out of the house. Papa B believed me, but nobody else did."

"Papa B?" She raised an eyebrow at the weird name.

"My grandpa. We called him Papa B. His real name was Barry."

Jaime savored the next bite of her fluffy waffle. "Did you ever see the mysterious ghost again?"

"No, and I tried. I read everything I found about ghost hunting and the tech they used. Made my own homemade EMF detector when I was twelve and tried to track down that ghost. Either the detector didn't work, or he was passing through." He leaned closer. "I like to think it was the latter. My tech never fails."

"Never?" She didn't believe a word.

"Never." Drew gave his most innocent expression. It made his hazel eyes larger. "Well, it takes a few tweaks, but then it works perfectly."

"I'm sure."

They ate in silence for a while until Drew broke it.

"How did you wind up in Asheville?"

Jaime pushed away her empty plate before sliding back in the booth. "Blackwood has a great history program, my college friend Layne and her husband are here, and it was something different." She tucked a strand of hair behind her ear. "After I had Ella, I felt stuck in Cary. It felt like all my dreams crumbled around my ears." Her head snapped up. "Don't misunderstand me. I love my daughter with my whole heart. But I was nineteen, and a new mom. I watched all my friends moving forward, and I stayed stuck in the same place."

"I can't imagine what that must have been like." Drew scooped some scrambled eggs onto his fork. "What does Ella think of Asheville?"

Joy filled Jaime's heart. Not one guy she ever dated before thought to ask about her daughter, but Drew always seemed interested. "Ella loves it here. It was hard for her to leave Cary and her grandparents and great grandparents. The whole extended family. But she's settled in and made friends." Jaime sighed, familiar guilt settling in. "My mom still likes to ask why I took her granddaughter all the way to the mountains. The way she puts it, I ripped Ella away from her family."

"I know what you mean about standing still." He shoved the eggs on his fork into his mouth. He chewed and swallowed before speaking again. "Well, not the kid part, but I didn't know what I wanted to do after college. I earned a computer science degree but had no desire to go out to California and work for any of those tech companies. Tristan took off for Wilmington for a few years. Zack..." He stopped for a moment and swallowed. "Sorry, it still hurts to think about Zack."

Jaime touched his arm. "He was the one who died three months ago?"

"Yeah." He wiped at his eyes and sighed. He chuckled. "I'm being weird. Sorry about that." He cleared his throat. "Anyway, he and Kayla moved here. I spent some time living at home with my mom, which was great, but I couldn't stay there forever. I found a job at a small tech company in Charlotte but wasn't happy.

"That's where I met Aaron. He came in searching for a tech guy for his paranormal investigation business. I said yes and followed him to Asheville."

Silence hovered over the table.

"You only lived with your mom?" Jaime ventured. "Was your dad around?" Drew scrunched his nose when she mentioned his father. For a minute, she wondered if she needed to back away from the subject, but curiosity got the better of her. She wanted to know everything about Drew.

"He wasn't the greatest dad and was mostly out of the picture for my teens. I'll leave it at that." He asked the waitress for the check.

"I'm sorry. I didn't mean to touch on a sore subject. Ella's dad never came around." She studied the table.

"Was he there in the beginning?"

She lifted her head, meeting his eyes. "No. Wasn't even at the hospital. When I told him I was pregnant, he transferred schools."

"Sounds like an asshole." Drew narrowed his eyes.

"He turned out to be."

The light mood quickly went south, and it seemed like a cloud covered the whole booth. Drew paid, leaving a generous tip. They walked back out onto the sidewalk. The temperature warmed but not enough to kill the chill in the air. She huddled further into her coat. Cold November days in Asheville reminded her of a crisp, homey feeling. Not like the stabbing ice that accompanied the ghost when he appeared in her house. *No, not thinking about him today.* Restless Spirits confiscated the fiddle. She didn't have to think about him ever again. She shoved the thought away and threaded her arm through Drew's. He beamed down at her.

She bumped his hip. "If you could see one band in concert, what would it be?"

Drew blinked down at her. The cloud seemed to lift from his eyes. "Black Sabbath, hands down."

"Old school metal, huh?" She grinned.

"The original. Why? Who would you want to see?"

Jaime tapped the end of her chin as she considered the question. "Probably Tori Amos."

Drew clutched his chest and stumbled back, dragging Jaime with him. He pressed his back against a brick wall. "Tori Amos? Really? You hurt me." He tapped the center of his chest. "Right here."

"What's wrong with Tori Amos?" Jaime stood her ground. "She's good, you know."

He groaned as he pulled her closer, and the world around her went quiet. It was like everything stopped moving. Cars passing and people talking faded into the background. Jaime met his eyes. Her heart beat faster as everything seemed to slow down.

She took his hat off to run her fingers through the short, blondish-brown locks. She then pressed her lips to his. She started the kiss soft and tentative at first, then she dove in, pulling him closer. He kissed her back with the same fervor. Electricity zipped down to the tips of her toes.

She enclosed her arms around his neck as the kiss deepened. She met his rhythm, slow and steady. She didn't feel the cold, nor did she notice the people walking past them. All she knew was this moment and this man.

After a while, Jaime broke the kiss, taking in a deep breath. Suddenly, she didn't even need her coat anymore. Her skin heated. Drew's cheeks burned bright red, and she didn't think the cold caused it. One thing she loved about pale men was that she could tell when they enjoyed something. The blood rushed to their faces, like it did to Drew's, as if the bulge in his pants weren't an indicator.

"Wow," he said.

"Yeah, wow."

Drew smiled, cradled her face, and kissed her back. It stole her breath away.

"Do we both need to go to work?" Drew asked when they came up for air.

"It'd be irresponsible of us not to." But Jaime tossed around different ways to play hooky in her head. Unfortunately, the responsible side of her won the inner battle. "I have to go. Not only do I have to teach, but Ella will want me to pick her up after school. And then I have to go back to Blackwood and take a class. I lead a complicated life."

Drew groaned again. "You're right. Someone has to go through the footage from your house last night, and Aaron won't like it if I'm not there." He traced a finger along her jawline. "Want to pick this up later tonight?"

Jaime bit her lip, considering the offer. "I can't. This will be Ella's first night back in her room. But I'd love for you to come with us to the antique store tomorrow afternoon."

"The antique store?"

"Yeah, I wanted to ask the lady who sold me the fiddle more about the star-crossed lovers' story. I meant to do it today, but you know." She stepped closer. "Time got away from me."

"I forgot all about that story." Drew tightened his hold around her waist. "I'm kind of curious now myself." He pressed his forehead to hers. "Sure you can't stay?"

"I'm sorry. The rest of the day calls." She dropped her arms from around his neck, already regretting the move. He opened his arms. She stumbled back and turned to head to the library parking garage.

"Hey, Jaime! Wait!"

She paused and faced him. "Yeah?"

"I need my hat back."

She lifted her hand, surprised to find she still held his Blue Devils cap. When she handed it back to him, he caught her hand in his.

"One more for the road?" He tipped her chin.

"Thought you'd never ask."

He swept her away in another kiss.

Pounding metal rang in his ears as Drew danced down the sidewalk. The noon sun didn't do much to chase away the wind's bite, but he didn't mind the cold. Everything fell into place in his world.

She kissed him. Or maybe she kissed him four times. Okay, they participated in a heavy make out session on the side of a building. Drew didn't remember the last time he felt that happy. Was this what love felt like? He thought about the previous women he dated. None of them compared to Jaime. Light burned brighter. Sounds echoed clearer. The air tasted sweeter. Everything seemed a little bit better.

He bounced into the office.

McKenna beamed at him, pointing at her ears. He paused the metal and removed his headphones.

Leaning forward, she rested her chin on her fist. "Someone's in a good mood."

"Mac, aren't you supposed to ask?" Drew fought the heat in his cheeks as he stuffed his headphones into his bag.

"I'm not scanning your emotions. It's all over your face. But if you'd like me to, I can."

"No, I'm good." He walked past her desk. "Just feeling better."

"Good to see the effects of last night didn't linger. Oh, Aaron is already going through the recordings. Tabitha will be in a little later."

Drew bit down on his snarky response. He wasn't a fan of Aaron hanging out in his office, but the man did own the business. If only Aaron had told him he was going to be in earlier. He sighed, letting his initial reaction go. "Thanks, Mac."

He started to walk past the closed conference room door when goose bumps broke out across his skin. His mood plummeted as a sense of dread settled inside of him. It weighed him down like an anchor. He caught sight of the closed conference room door. It tugged at him as if it begged him to open it. He drifted to it and did so without giving it a second thought.

The fiddle lay in the middle of the conference room table with a circle of salt around it. It glowed and pulsed as he stepped into the room.

"Let me out," a faint voice whispered.

Drew reached toward the salt.

"Drew?" McKenna caught his arm. "What are you doing?"

He blinked. "I don't know." He took a shaky step back. "You put it in the conference room?"

"The door was locked." He whirled to see McKenna messing with the knob. "Or it was."

"Because no ghost or demon has ever been able to go through a locked door." The fiddle continued to shine. "Or apparently make someone unlock it without realizing it." He now felt the cool metal of the key in his hand. A key he didn't remember pulling from his pocket.

McKenna stood beside him and rested a hand on his

shoulder. "So much anger and hate, and I can't read the emotions of an object."

"I think you're zeroing in on what's in the object."

She set her jaw, her eyes unfocusing. "He wants you dead so badly. He…blames you?" She grabbed Drew's hand, yanking him from the room. She then closed and locked the door behind them. "Whatever or whoever's in that fiddle is evil. Pure, black evil."

"Did you feel any of this when you put it in there?" Drew backed away from the door as far as he could. The urge to go back sang in his blood even though he was almost to his own office door.

"Aaron was the one who put it in there, and no. I didn't feel anything until you got close to it." She moved away from the door. "Clearly, either we need to get rid of it, or you have to work from home." She faced him. "Will you be okay?"

"Yeah."

"Are you sure?" She took a step toward him. "You're fighting not to go back over there."

Drew wiped the sweat off his brow. His breathing increased. "Can you block it somehow?"

"I don't know. I can try." She closed her eyes, and the irresistible call lessened. Drew took a cleansing breath as his skin cooled. He stuffed his shaking hands into his pockets. McKenna opened her eyes, but there was a strain on her face. "It's strong, Drew. I don't know how long I can hold it off."

"Maybe I'll be fine in my office. Just hold it long enough for me to get there." He dropped his set of keys to the office in her hand. "And keep these, just in case."

"Okay."

He nodded a thanks to McKenna as he dashed into his small space. The draw went up a notch as soon as he closed the door. He thought she must have let go. But it no longer tore at him as bad as it had been. Drew pressed a hand to his door, praying he would make it through the day.

"I was wondering when you were going to show. Haven't heard anything on the recordings yet." A chair scraped along the floor. "You alright?"

Drew whirled, pushing his back to the door. Aaron studied him with concerned brown eyes.

"The fiddle keeps pulling at me, even in that circle of salt."

Aaron's eyebrows shot up. "Really?" He tugged his headphones all the way off. "I'll add more salt. Tell me if that helps."

Drew moved aside, and Aaron slipped out.

Drew breathed in and out slowly. His fingernails dug into the palms of his hands. The fiddle didn't entice him as strong as the night before, but it drilled into his soul. If he had any doubts about his connection to it, they had vanished into thin air. Every fiber in his being wanted to destroy the salt circle and let the smoke shadow demon smother him.

He stared at the computer monitor in front of him and thought of Jaime. Her smile, her eyes, her hair, her laugh, her everything. Latching onto an image of her eased the fiddle's grip on him. He focused all of his attention on her. The pull lessened and lessened until it became a quiet buzz in the back of his mind.

His door creaked open.

"I moved it out back to the alley behind us. Did that help?" Aaron poked his head in.

Drew let go of Jaime's image and concentrated on the strange siren song. It hovered in the back of his mind, buzzing like a bee, but not as intense before. His shoulders relaxed as he dropped his bag on the floor.

"Better. Much better." He peeled away from the wall. "Much, much better."

An hour later, the fiddle forgotten, Drew stared at a computer monitor. Tabitha and Aaron in grayscale wandered around Ella's room. Tabitha pointed an EMF detector at every wall and corner while Aaron talked into a tape recorder. Nothing else happened.

Drew suspected this camera contained footage of people walking in and out of the room but no ghosts. Aaron said nothing happened in the room, but a part of him hoped the technology caught something their eyes didn't see. He straightened his legs and let the footage continue for a few more seconds. After that, he called that one a bust. He removed his headphones and rubbed his dry, tired eyes.

He nudged Aaron's shoulder. "Anything on the tapes?"

Aaron moved one of his headphones. "Right now, nothing but regular conversation and a lot of dead air." His jaw twitched. "I guess this means the activity in the living room was all that happened. You still got it on your phone?"

Drew connected his phone to the monitor and selected the footage. "I hope so. I haven't watched it since I shot it." He considered it the night before, but the encounter still rattled him. The smoky shadow's icy touch and deep voice lingered in Drew's memory.

"Play it. Maybe you caught something you didn't notice. Something we can use to make sure we got the right object. I don't want that kid to go back into that house and face those ghosts again."

"Me, neither." He didn't realize what Ella had been through until the shadow sucked almost all of his air. Another idea occurred to him. Why had the other ghost protected Ella, but not jumped to his defense? He kept the question in his mind as he started the footage.

Tristan stood in the middle of the screen, already in the

throes of his vision. The fiddle glowed behind him. Drew watched himself prop the phone on the side table and pluck the shining fiddle off the wall. Then, plain as day, the ghost filled half of the frame, begging for help. The screen went black right before the recording stopped.

Drew backed up to the point where the phone recorded the ghost and paused it.

"Well, I'll be," Aaron stared at the screen, his mouth hanging open. "I've never caught a clear full-body apparition on a recording before. Not once." He smacked Drew on the back hard. Drew winced. "That's amazing! Play it again and turn up the sound. I want to hear every word he says."

Drew pressed play.

His screen self and the ghost studied each other. Same height, same build.

"Please help me. Help me find my treasure." Each word held a heavy amount of static, but he made out every syllable. Then Tristan screamed off camera. Drew turned away, but the ghost still floated in the same spot. The man hung his head. "I'm sorry. He's coming." Then he vanished before the shadow covered everything, and the recording stopped.

"Jaime reported the same conversation." Drew rubbed his chin. "He seemed defeated when he knew the shadow was coming."

"But we don't have anything new," Aaron protested.

"Maybe not on camera, but I remembered something. The ghost saved Ella. He stood between her and the shadow when we got the door open."

"Okay."

"The ghost didn't protect me."

Aaron crossed his arms and leaned back. "You're right. He left you high and dry."

"Why?" Drew drummed his fingers on the desk. "Why protect Ella, but throw me to the wolves, so to speak?"

"That's a good question. I wish I had an answer." Aaron reached into the pocket of his shirt and let out a groan. "It's times like these I wish I hadn't quit smoking." Drew knew the agonizing details of how Tabitha convinced Aaron to quit cigarettes a month earlier. Aaron made sure everyone in the office heard.

Drew rested his head on his hand, defeat filling every pore. How could the rest of the day after such an amazing kiss go so completely downhill? First the fiddle, and now this. He found nothing new to help solve this case, and he realized that the ghost wanted Ella protected more than him. What was he to the apparition? Chopped liver?

Aaron settled the headphones back on his ears and pressed play. He sat back in the chair, his arms crossed and his eyes closed. A minute hadn't passed when his eyes flew open. He hit pause.

The headphones came off again as he turned wide eyes on Drew.

"What?" The scrutiny bore into him.

"I didn't realize I left the tape recorder going when we came running." Aaron pulled the headphone cord out of the jack, rewound, and hit play. The shadow's eerie, raspy voice played through the speakers.

"Give up, boy. Give in. You're mine. Give in to me. I knew I'd find you, and you'll die like the rest."

A chill ran down Drew's spine. He got to his feet, inching away from the speakers. Even now, the icy cold seemed to snake around him and squeeze.

Aaron raised an eyebrow as he hit pause. "You weren't kidding when you said you thought the shadow wanted you." He flattened his lips into a straight line.

"No, I wasn't." Drew took a deep breath. "I looked up my family on one of those ancestry sites to see if I could make a connection. All they had was Keane, born in Ireland." Then he remembered Jaime's revelation. "Jaime said she dreamed about my great-great grandmother, and she told Jaime she needed to save him. We thought she meant the ghost."

"Wait." Aaron held up a hand. "Is Jaime psychic like her daughter?"

"No. That's the weird thing. She was with me at the library this morning, and we saw a picture of my great-great grandmother, Melinda. She swore it was the woman in her dream."

Aaron stood. "Why didn't you tell me the minute you got here?"

"I didn't think about it."

"Drew."

"I swear. We had the weird thing with the fiddle, and then we got to work."

Aaron grabbed his shoulders. "Drew, has anyone else in your family died under mysterious circumstances?"

"I don't know." Fear crept along Drew's spine. "I don't know the Keane side of the family that well."

Aaron let go of him. "I suggest you find out because it sounds to me like you and Jaime might be cursed."

"Cursed?" Drew backed into the wall. "Curses aren't real. They can't be. Ghosts can't curse people, can they?"

"I hate to disappoint you, but curses are real. I've dealt with them a couple of times before." Aaron sat on the edge of the desk. His hand went to the pocket of his jeans. He swore when he remembered he didn't have a cigarette. He yanked out a stick of nicotine gum and chewed furiously. "The only way to stop this is to break the curse, and that's the direction we need to take."

Drew crossed the room and sank into his chair. A curse? Someone or something cursed him? He dragged Jaime into this? His heart sank. Whatever was happening to him, he didn't want to bring Jaime into it.

"I'm going to get some air." Aaron walked out of the office, leaving Drew alone with his thoughts.

The air cooled around him. Goosebumps popped up on his flesh. Drew rubbed his arms. "It's all in your head," he muttered.

The monitor on his desk popped and went dark. A wire sparked. The lightbulb in his lamp burst, plunging the whole room into darkness. Ice and inky blackness surrounded him.

"Now, where did we leave off?" the shadow growled in his ear.

1 2

Drew pushed against the dark, his heart pounding in his chest. *Not again! Not again!* He fumbled for the door knob. When his hand landed on it, he twisted and turned, but the door didn't budge. An unseen force held it in place. His hands shook.

"I'm not done, boy. I won't be done until every last one of you is dead." The black smoke filled Drew's mouth, nose, and lungs.

He tried to breathe, to move. Spots danced in front of his eyes. He clawed and fought, but his hands passed through the cold smoke. He had to think, to do something, but the black shadow pinned him in place.

This was it. He knew he would die in his own office. He fell backward, his chair landing on the hard floor with a clatter. He crab walked to the wall, freeing himself enough to take in a breath of air. The walls of the tiny office closed in on every side.

"Why?" he pushed out.

"Why? You deserve it. He stole what was mine. I'll take everything from him." The smoke writhed and coiled around him like a snake. It solidified, squeezing around Drew's throat. His vision darkened and narrowed to a small point of light.

Drew flailed, his hand hitting the edge of his desk and smacked something hard and curved. Feeling around, he made out the gun's shape. His fingers closed around the handle. The disruptor. The disruptor that didn't work. He grabbed it anyway, praying it had spent the night recharging. He flipped the switch on the side, and the disruptor buzzed to life, its mechanics whirring. He pointed and shot. Every bit of his equipment went dead as his machine punched a hole through the smoke.

Drew lay on the cold floor, his body weakening. In the distance, he heard pounding on the door. One thud. Another thud.

The smoke eased a little. It receded enough for Drew to draw in sweet, sweet air. But the shadow repaired its hole, regrouped, and coiled around him once more. It continued to squeeze the life out of him.

After one more thud, a square of light poured into the room. A hail of salt rained down on him, covering everything in white. He tasted the grains on the tip of his tongue. The shadow fought it. More salt joined the first batch. With a screech, the blackness broke apart and disappeared.

Drew sucked cool air into his lungs. He rested his cheek on the welcome freezing hard floor. He planned to lie there forever. He noticed the rawness around his throat as he tried to move his weak muscles.

Aaron crouched next to him, the salt can in his hand. "Are you okay?"

"Yeah, that shadow definitely wants me dead." He met Aaron's concerned eyes. "You might be onto something with this whole cursed thing."

For the second time, Drew found himself at a table with a glass of water in his hand. The constant ghostly punching bag routine ruffled his temper. But this time, he knew the ghost didn't attack because he was in the way. This ghost, shadow, demon, whatever the hell it was, set its sights on him specifically.

McKenna sat across from him, glaring at the fiddle in the middle of the table. "We have to destroy this thing. There's got to be a way to break the curse. I can't believe the shadow broke out of the salt circle and attacked you right here in the office." Her brows drew together, her jaw clenched. Drew couldn't read emotions like she could, but he knew she was pissed.

"I wouldn't be surprised if others have tried." Aaron paced around the room. Every so often, he reached into his shirt pocket and pulled out nothing. A swear word or a colorful phrase followed close behind. He then snatched a pack of gum from another pocket, popping a stick into his mouth.

Tabitha drummed her purple-painted nails on the table's surface. "I bet my family would have something to destroy it with."

"No! N-O! I'm not going to them for a damn thing!" *Chomp, chomp, chomp* on the gum. "You know how I feel about the Greene Institute."

Everyone knew how Aaron felt about his former place of employment. The Greene Institute for Paranormal Research was a large operation down in Charlotte, and the place where Aaron and Tabitha learned their trade. But they never explained why they had left or why Aaron didn't trust them.

Drew watched all of this as if following a TV show. Everything happened around him, and he soaked it all in without participating. His earlier fear left him hollow and numb. He sipped his water while he stared at the fiddle. Again, he wondered why a shadow attached itself to it and why it hated him so much. The shadow had said something about taking everything from him. Who? The other ghost? And how did Drew's death accomplish that goal? He thought about the other ghost, the one with eyes like his, and the possible family connection.

He set down his glass as a realization struck him.

"Where was the other ghost?"

Everyone in the room stopped and looked at him.

"What?" Aaron snapped.

Drew surveyed the faces of his co-workers and friends. "The other ghost. The blond man in the overalls and the hat. The one that looks human. He appeared first before each attack, but he didn't appear this time. Why?"

Everyone exchanged glances.

"That is strange." Tabitha leaned back in her chair. "Maybe he completely became the shadow?"

Drew shook his head. "No. They feel like two different spirits."

"What do you mean?" McKenna's voice was soft.

Drew pulled off his hat, setting it next to him, and scratched his head. "I don't know how to explain it. The shadow gives off a cold, deathly vibe. The ghost didn't feel like that." He scratched his chin, trying to find the words. "He seems earnest, hopeful." He met McKenna's eyes. "Have you done any research on the fiddle?"

"A little. You and Jaime found it at the shop up the street, right? Mountain Peak Antiques? I planned on going by there this afternoon."

"Jaime wanted to go ask questions there tomorrow. You said you did a little. What did you find?"

"Nothing really pops up online about this particular fiddle. It hasn't left a legend or a trail of deaths in its wake."

"Interesting." Tabitha lifted a brow. "A killer shadow is attached to this object, and it hasn't killed everyone who's ever owned it?"

Drew's back twinged with a sharp jolt of pain when he jerked. He winced, noticing he hit the floor harder than he thought. "I think he's looking for particular family members. He said he won't stop until every last one of us was dead."

"Us?" Aaron straightened.

"No. I think he meant my family, specifically. He wants revenge on me."

He cleared his throat as he regarded his co-workers, his friends. "I know you want to research this thing, but I think we should try to stop the shadow." He nodded to Aaron. "McKenna was right. We've got to try to destroy the fiddle."

"Alright." Aaron hooked a thumb in the pocket of his jeans. "It's worth a try. You got a hammer in your toolbox back there?"

"Never know when you might need one."

"Good. Grab it, and let's give it a try."

Drew took a deep breath before dashing back into his office. He couldn't shake the cold fear running through him, but he refused to let some shadow ghost scare him out of his sanctuary. He supposed Tristan felt the same way when The White Lady stalked his apartment. He dug out a hammer and made his way back to the conference table.

He gripped the handle, the heft in his hand weighing him down. "Stand back."

Aaron, McKenna, and Tabitha scuttled away from the table.

Drew lifted the hammer and swung down. It hit the center of the fiddle with a loud crack. He wielded it again. The wood splintered apart, pieces flying across the table. He kept wrecking it until the fiddle was nothing more than broken wood and strings.

"Get some salt," Drew said.

Tabitha ducked out of the room and came back with a whole can of salt. Drew dumped almost all of it on the fiddle.

"I feel like there should be more," Tabitha commented.

McKenna narrowed her eyes. "That was too easy."

As soon as she spoke, the broken pieces slid across the table all on their own. They joined together, fusing and knitting. Each piece seemed to shake off the salt. The strings reattached themselves. Right before Drew's astonished eyes, the fiddle put itself back together.

"Oh, my God," McKenna breathed.

"That's not fucking normal." Aaron bent down for a closer look.

Tabitha covered her mouth with her hand.

A laugh echoed around them.

Drew gripped the back of the nearest chair. "So, that's how it's going to be." He gritted his teeth. "Let's salt and burn the damn thing."

"Not in the middle of my office," Aaron declared. "But I agree with you. The problem is we don't have anywhere to burn it."

Drew kicked the chair and stalked to the wall. "There has to be somewhere."

McKenna edged her way out of the room. "I'm on it."

Whatever it took, Drew declined to let a possessed fiddle win. He prepared to fight with everything he had inside of him.

***

If the fiddle couldn't be destroyed, and they couldn't find an easy place to burn it, Drew decided to dig further into his family tree. Although he considered that the ghost was his father's ancestor, he wanted to talk to his mother instead.

His grandfather passed away two years earlier, and he didn't know any relatives on the Keane side well enough to ask them about the ghost or the fiddle. So he hoped his mother possessed the answers. He would do anything to avoid talking to his father.

After two rings, his mother answered the video call. A beautiful older lady with frosted, short hair and bright blue eyes appeared in the center of the frame. Her whole expression brightened. "My heart! Now my day got a whole lot better." She waved.

"Hi, Mom." Drew tilted forward, waving and chuckling. "You don't have to wave every time we chat face to face on the computer."

Sara Daulton tossed her head back, laughing. "I know, silly, but I like doing it. You do it right back to me."

"You're tan already. How's the cruise?"

"It's fantastic! Greg and I are having the best time. We even tried scuba diving yesterday. You should've seen me. You'd be proud." Drew's mom settled back in her reclining chair, so she appeared at an angle. "Anyway, look at this view!" She twirled her phone away from her to show the edge of the deck and the blue water beyond. After a few minutes, she returned to the frame.

"It's gorgeous! Did I catch you at a bad time?" Drew loved the fact his mother had met a great guy that treated her the way she deserved to be treated. His dad bullied her for years before she found the courage to grab Drew and his older sister Lori and walk out. Drew could tell she was enjoying her late fifties.

"Absolutely not. I always have time for you." She rolled onto her side. "Now, what's going on?"

Drew cleared his throat. He hadn't quite planned out how to ask his mother about a possible ghost in the family. She knew all about his job as a paranormal investigator and supported it one hundred percent. But this topic was something different.

"Well, it's a little weird." He winced as his voice cracked on the last word.

Sara tensed and moved her phone closer to her. A worried expression replaced her earlier mirth. "What is it? What's wrong? Were you in the hospital again? Do I need to come home?"

She would, too. All he had to do was say the word, and his mother would find a way to get to Asheville even if she had to swim the ocean herself.

"No. I'm fine. We're all fine. I just have a weird question to ask you." He rubbed his palms on his jeans.

"Shoot. I love weird questions." She settled down again.

"Have you ever heard any family stories about a fiddle or a ghost looking for treasure?" He laid the query out in the open. Saying it out loud made it feel all too real.

Sara tapped her chin. "Not that I know of, but the fiddle part sounds familiar." She gasped and covered her mouth, her eyes wide. "Was there a sort of shadow?" Her voice trembled as she asked.

Drew opened his mouth. Of all the reactions he expected, that wasn't one of them. "You know about the shadow?"

"I'm coming home." Sara grabbed one end of her towel.

"Mom, no. I can handle this. It's my job. Tell me everything you know about the shadow."

Sara clutched the towel in one hand, fraying the edge with her thumb. "It happened before Lori or you ever came along. Before..." she paused and swallowed. "Before your father's drinking got out of hand."

"Go on."

"We had just gotten married and were staying at your Uncle Charlie's house." She took a breath.

"Uncle Charlie? Didn't he die before I was born?" Drew didn't like the direction this conversation headed in.

"He did." She laid her towel over the back of the chair and smoothed it out. "Anyway, he had this fiddle in his house, said it was a family heirloom. Well, one night, I got up to get something to drink. Something cold and black passed over me. The room went dark for a moment, and I swear I heard a deep laugh." She smoothed the towel, avoiding Drew's eyes. "I turned around and a black shadow blocked the window. It was a mass of darkness."

"What happened, Mom?" Drew perched on the edge of his couch. Both of his parents were alive and well. He knew the shadow didn't hurt either one of them, but he suspected his uncle hadn't been so lucky.

"It was there for a moment, and then it was gone. Lights came back on. It looked like nothing had happened."

"Did you tell anybody?"

"I asked your uncle about it the next day. He said it was nothing and not to worry about it."

Drew rubbed his chin as he absorbed the information. "Did he say anything else?"

"No, we left that day." She covered her mouth. "I always heard your father's cousins say they didn't think Charlie's death was an accident."

"How did you know it was the fiddle?"

"One of your father's cousins said she saw it glow once, and they immediately got rid of it after Charlie died." Sara's brows dipped. "I take it the fiddle found you?"

He wasn't quite sure what to call Jaime, so he settled on something simple. "A woman I know bought it at an antique shop."

"I think your father asked his family about the fiddle once, but they never liked talking about it. It wouldn't hurt to talk to him, honey." Sara spread out her towel and placed it over her legs.

"I'd rather not talk to him."

His mother sighed as she settled back into her lounge chair. "I wish you and your father had a better relationship. If I hadn't taken you away, maybe it would be better."

"Mom, it's not your fault. It's Dad's. He was the one who wrecked our relationship, not you."

"But still. He wasn't the same after his brother died, you know." She tapped her fingernails on the arm of the chair.

"He didn't have to drink. There's always another choice." It hurt like hell when Zack died, but Drew still chose to stay far away from hard liquor. Getting drunk didn't make the pain go away.

Sara blinked and forced a smile. "Tell me something good so we don't end on this low note."

He recognized the tactic. She used it to bring a conversation back to the positive. He appreciated it and always had, even if he didn't tell her. "I almost got my ghost disruptor working. It disrupted all the ghosts, and all the electricity, too. I'm going to have to figure something else out."

This time, she smiled for real, the twinkle back in her eyes. "You're going to get it right next time. I know it."

"I hope so." Jaime popped into Drew's thoughts along with the memory of her kiss. He debated whether or not to tell his mother about her. Even though they had been dating for a while, neither one of them declared anything official...but that kiss. It felt right, more right than anything else had in a long time. "I met someone," he blurted before he thought better of it.

"Oh?" Sara straightened, pure joy on her face.

"Her name is Jaime. It isn't serious yet."

"But you like her?"

"I think so. Yeah."

Sara clapped. "Then I can't wait to meet her."

"We aren't at that stage yet, Mom."

She waved her hand. "But I'm not like other moms. I'm not judgey or uptight. I'm cool."

"Mom. You're breaking up."

She rolled her eyes. "Fine. Leave your mother out. I only brought you into this world."

"Mom." Drew chuckled at the old joke.

"I love you, my heart. Please be careful with the ghosts and the fiddle. And talk to your father. He'd have the most insight."

"We'll see. Love you, Mom."

D o you see anything?"

Ella clutched her phone as she crept into her room. She flicked on the light, taking in all the familiar objects. Her comfortable bed with her purple comforter. The movie and pop star posters that adorned the walls. All of the little objects, like music boxes and tiny statues, she liked to collect. All remained quiet and still.

"No ghosts. Looks like it's all clear." She turned the phone so her best friend Kelly McHone could see the room, too.

She didn't mean to tell Kelly about the ghost. It came out during a conversation at lunch. Instead of calling her a weirdo, Kelly grew excited. She wanted to know everything about the ghost. So Ella told her, leaving out any reference to her psychic ability, of course. She wasn't ready to trust Kelly that much yet.

She turned the phone back to face her.

"Looks clear to me, too. Sure you don't want to sleepover at my house?" Kelly's green eyes widened. "Or I can sleep at yours." Her pale face beamed too much at that idea.

"I wish you could stay here tonight, but Mom won't let

me have a sleepover on a school night." How unfair! Her mom and Layne basically held sleepovers for most of the week, and Mom didn't allow Ella to invite any friends over on a school night.

But at least she had moved back into her own room again.

Someone yelled at Kelly off screen. She glanced in the person's direction, her blonde curls bouncing. "I've got to go do homework." She rolled her eyes. "Talk to you tomorrow."

"See you then." Ella ended the call and sat down on her soft bed.

Silence hung in the room.

Mom had explained that the ghost hunters took the ghosts away with the fiddle and that she didn't have to worry anymore. She hadn't lied about the fiddle. Ella didn't see it on the living room wall, and she didn't hear the low tone it seemed to make whenever she stood near it. With most objects, she learned to tune out their sounds, but the fiddle hummed right there in her ears. And the tone sounded like off pitch moaning, too. But she no longer heard it. The objects she knew hummed the only tones left in the house.

She considered playing some real music to make herself feel better and to push away the quiet. She opened her music app, choosing a pop song with a bouncy beat. As it filled the room, Ella let out a sigh of relief. Everything was going to be okay. She threw herself back on the bed and closed her eyes. She lay in her room. She prepared to reclaim it. Her sanctuary.

A new tune wove itself around the notes of the song. At first, Ella didn't notice, but then it got louder, playing counterpoint to the other song. It sounded high-pitched and sad, like an instrument crying. Ella's eyes flew open. The ghosts weren't back, were they? She cut off the music as she sat up. Cold air didn't fill the room, and her lights burned bright. But the high-pitched song continued.

She slid off the bed and walked around her room. She checked under the bed, inside her closet, in all of her drawers. The music never changed. Normally, when she got close to an object, its song grew louder. When she moved away, it played softer. But this song stayed the same.

An image flashed in her mind of a long, wooden box. She saw it clearly, even though wherever it rested was in a dark place. The music stopped as abruptly as it started.

Ella swallowed as she gripped the edge of her desk. Nothing like that had ever happened before. She heard objects when she remained in the same room with them. Visions of random things didn't pop into her head. She performed another frantic search, looking for the same box she had seen, but she didn't find it anywhere in her room.

She dashed into the hall and searched that closet. Nothing. She ran into her mother's room. She glanced under the bed and in the closet and even her mother's drawers. No long, wooden box. She raced downstairs to find her mom stretched out on the couch with a book in her hands.

"Well, hey, there." Mom's smile faded when she looked at Ella. She slammed the book shut. "What is it? What's wrong?"

"I hear an object, but I can't find it." The whole situation scared her. Her power made her weird, and now something had changed, something she couldn't explain. She clutched her stomach, trying to calm the twisting.

Mom dropped her feet to the floor. "Do you hear it now? Where is the sound coming from?"

"No. I heard it in my room and then I saw it in my head. It's a long, wooden box." Ella's voice rose an octave. Her stomach continued to churn. "Mom, it's not here. It's not in my room. It's not upstairs. And it stopped singing after I saw it." Ella felt a lump in her throat. She fought to not cry. Only little kids cried. Not big girls. She pushed so hard against it, but her vision swam. "Mom?"

Mom pulled her into a hug, and Ella let a sob escape. She was safe. Mom wasn't going to let anything happen to her. "It's okay. It's okay. We can figure this out."

Cold prickled Ella's skin. But the chill held a comfort to it. It started small, an awareness crawling along the back of her neck. Ella gasped. She peered over her Mom's arm. The ghost appeared right next to them. Not the shadow, but the ghost who tried to protect her. He looked the same, with his overalls and his hat. His sad eyes regarded them.

"What do you want?" Mom's voice held a tough edge, but it shook a little.

"Please, you have to help me. You have to find my treasure." His voice sounded clearer this time. He had a strange accent, like the Lucky Charms leprechaun. "I know you and your little one can do it." He took a step forward and his lower half disappeared into the coffee table.

"What treasure?"

"You've got to find it, lass. It's the only way to stop him." He lowered his head.

Ella gripped her mother tighter. Even though she knew this ghost wouldn't hurt her, the bad ghost probably didn't linger far behind.

"Stop who? The shadow?"

The ghost gave no indication he heard her. "Find my treasure and stop him. He's already trying to kill the boy." He paused. "My boy." Ella never heard the ghost talk so much. He seemed to glow brighter. "Please, help me before it's too late. He'll kill him." With those parting words, he vanished into nothing.

———

Jaime spent two hours soothing Ella and getting her into bed. She lay next to her daughter until the girl drifted off to sleep.

Jaime breathed in and let the air out slowly. She thought her house belonged to her again. No more ghost. No more shadow. No more fiddle. She had been a little sad about the fiddle, though. It was such a pretty handmade piece. But she refused to keep it if ghosts and shadows tormented Ella. Even though the shadow didn't appear, it seemed like the ghost decided to hang around. How did he do that if he was attached to the fiddle, and Drew's team took the fiddle away?

She reflected on the rest of the day, which went well otherwise. Her students acted restless, but they paid attention to her lecture. Thanksgiving break was three weeks away, so she didn't blame them, but they still had plenty of material to cover before the end of the semester. She couldn't say the same for her own attention in the classes she attended.

Ella beamed when she had picked her up from school. She chatted all the way home about how Mrs. Brenner chose her drawing of a fruit bowl to show as an example to the whole class.

Dinner and the rest of the evening went by like normal. She and Ella had moved back home and resumed their normal routine. And then came Ella's reaction and the ghost. Everything had tumbled downhill from there.

After their ghostly visitor disappeared, Ella drew the object she had seen.

"Mom." She shoved the sheet of paper into Jaime's hands. "I keep seeing and hearing this box."

A long, slim box with dirt and rocks surrounding it filled the page. Nothing looked familiar in the drawing.

"Where is it?" She sat on the edge of the couch, worry

churning in her stomach. Ella located missing objects near her; she didn't see them in places miles away. Tuning into an object that wasn't in the house was all new territory for both of them.

"I don't know. It's dark and damp." Ella shrugged. She pulled at a string on the white afghan that decorated the back of the couch. "It's wooden, like the old fiddle. Brown, I think. And it sings a high-pitched, slow song." She hummed a few bars of a song Jaime had never heard before. Ella told her about the tones and sounds other objects made, but hearing about this new aspect of her daughter's gift came across as strange. "I think we have to find it."

Jaime rubbed her daughter's arm. "Do you want to do that?"

Ella nodded. "I think we have to help him. He protected me from the shadow."

"He did, didn't he?" She tugged her daughter closer. She thought about her dream the previous night and wondered whether she should keep it from Ella or not. Hiding it from her daughter wasn't fair, not after Ella told her about the box. "You know, I think we're both a part of this. I had a weird dream the other night." She described the woman in the woods and everything the woman said about protecting someone. Ella seemed to take it all in.

"What do we do now?" Ella asked once Jaime finished.

"Well, I think we need to tell Drew and his friends everything we told each other and see if they can help us."

Ella wrinkled her nose. "Do we have to tell Drew? Can't it just be our thing?"

"What's wrong with Drew? I thought you liked him." Jaime knew her surprise probably showed all over her face.

"He's okay." Ella shrugged. "But he won't be around for long, right?"

Jaime leaned back, her mouth open. "Why do you say that?"

"The other guys didn't hang around for long."

How much attention did Ella pay to the few dates Jaime had been on? Even though she wanted to think of her daughter as a baby, she realized Ella acted like a young woman. A smart, perceptive one.

"Regardless, he still knows more about this ghost stuff than we do."

She thought about calling him after Ella fell asleep, but it was late, and Jaime found her own eyes closing.

"You're back with questions in your eyes." The redhead in the clearing brightened as Jaime stepped out of the forest. "We don't have a lot of time tonight." She patted the rocking chair next to her own, which sat on the front porch of a cottage that hadn't been there the last time. Jaime didn't see the baby.

Jaime climbed the creaky stairs and settled in next to her. "Where is your son?"

"Safe inside." She picked up her knitting needles and went back to the project she worked on. Jaime tilted forward, trying to make out what the project was. She noticed blue and green threaded through it but not what shape it formed. The redhead's needles clicked as she knitted.

If the woman was right, and they didn't have much time, Jaime didn't want to beat around the bush. "Is your name Melinda Beauchamp?"

"Melinda Keane, actually. I guess I didn't properly introduce myself." She smiled. "And you're Drew's Jaime."

"How did you know my name? How do you know Drew's name? How are you in my dream?" Even though she knew she was dreaming this time, everything felt so real. Her fingers ran along

smooth wood on the chair like last time. It creaked when she rocked. The dirt and trees gave off an earthy, damp smell. Melinda sat next to her, clear as day.

"Calm down now. One question at a time." Melinda lifted her eyes and grinned. "I don't rightly know how it all works, but I know your names because Drew is one of mine. And I'm in your dream because I just know I needed to be here." She gave Jaime a pointed look.

"What do you mean Drew is one of yours?"

"He comes from me. My husband and me. He's ours." She looped green yarn around her needles. "As you belong to your ancestors."

Jaime understood that sentiment. Family, especially ancestors, were important, and in her family, honored and respected.

"Who was your husband?" Jaime rocked, her skin warming from the pleasant sunshine.

The needles stilled as Melinda stared out across the clearing. "My Jeremiah, all the way from Dublin, Ireland. He didn't have a penny to his name, but I loved him anyway."

"Jeremiah Keane." Her ghost, who definitely had an Irish accent, possessed a name. Drew's great-great grandfather had a name unless her subconscious played tricks on her and she had created this in her head.

"Yes. Jeremiah Keane." Melinda went back to her knitting, her needles clicking in the silence.

Jaime took a moment to think of her next question. "The last time I was here, you said I had to protect him. Who is he?"

The needles and their clicking slowed. "I'm surprised you're asking. Why, Drew, of course. The darkness found him, and it wants him dead." A shadow crossed her features. "It's my fault."

"How?"

The needles paused, letting the silence take over. "I put them all in danger because I followed my heart."

Jaime stopped rocking and leaned forward. "You're going to have to give me more to go on."

A deep growl roared in the woods.

"It's not safe tonight." *Melinda packed her knitting and yarn.* "He's listening."

With that, Jaime woke to the sound of her alarm clock, more confused than ever.

Jaime squeezed Drew's free hand as she filled him in on Ella's ghostly visitor and the newest dream on the drive to Mountain Peak Antiques the next afternoon. She considered telling him about everything on the phone the first thing that morning, but the information needed more of an in-person conversation. She noted how his eyebrows rose when she told him his great-great grandfather was named Jeremiah.

"Of course, it was a dream, and it's possible I made up that name." She wanted to cover her bases since nothing made sense anymore.

Drew let go of her hand and made a left turn into the nearest parking garage. "But you did recognize her from the picture after the first dream."

"True." Jaime held her hands out to the heater, feeling her frozen fingers thaw. "But the biggest thing that confuses me is the fact that the ghost is still in my house."

"But you don't have the fiddle. How did he get there?"

Jaime shrugged. "I was hoping you'd know. Can a ghost

separate from the object it's attached to? This is all new territory for me."

"Me, too, actually. I'll have to ask Tabitha and Aaron." The car ascended to the next level of the deck. "Let me get this straight. The ghost, Jeremiah, wants us to find his treasure to stop the shadow from killing his kid. Melinda told you to keep an eye on me."

"Right." Jaime nodded.

Drew groaned as he selected a space and parked. "Aaron might be onto something with his curse theory." A long pause punctuated the sentence. "That fiddle has some sort of hold on me, and the shadow attacked me at work yesterday."

Jaime straightened, her whole body vibrating. "Drew, why didn't you tell me?"

"I'm telling you now." He rubbed the back of his neck like he always did when he didn't want to be completely honest.

"Are you okay?" She stroked his arm.

"Yeah, but I have to work from home until we can destroy the fiddle. Turns out you can't just chop it up. It'll put itself back together."

Jaime let the words sink in, a feeling of dread washing over her. "The fiddle put itself back together?" The structure of that sentence didn't seem right.

"Piece by piece. I watched the whole thing."

She swallowed. "Oh, my God." This story became stranger each passing minute. She tried to wrap her brain around the image of a self-mending fiddle, but she couldn't will herself to picture it.

"We're going to try to burn it next."

Jaime bit her bottom lip. "I don't think you should. Ella had a vision last night, and she doesn't get visions." She told Drew about the box and how Ella wanted to help the ghost. "I think whatever's in that box might be his treasure. I think we have to find it to end this." She tapped her chin with her forefinger. "Besides, if the fiddle can magically mend itself back together, what makes you think it can't unburn itself?"

"Fire can purify things. I have a lot of faith in it."

Jaime lifted a brow. "Don't you think someone would have tried that by now if they dealt with the ghosts we did?"

Drew cut off the engine. "Good point. Does Ella know where her mystery box is?"

"Not specifically. She drew a picture of where she thinks it is, but it's vague. No identifying marks anywhere." She unhooked her seatbelt, turning in her seat to face him. "Do you think McKenna might be willing to help her figure out where it is?"

"I know for a fact she'd love to. If she could start her own X-Men-style school for psychics, she would." Drew's sigh echoed through the car. "So I guess I'm working from home for the foreseeable future, huh?"

"At least until we find a way to break this curse."

Freezing air rushed in as he pushed open his door. "Maybe the lady at the antique store will give us a place to start?"

They entered the antique store and headed for the counter. Jaime peered at the assortment of items along the way, wishing she could spend hours looking through them. Of course, falling in love with an old object started this whole mess in the first place.

"Can I help you?" The young lady at the counter smiled at them.

"I hope so. I don't remember her name, but a woman with a long, brown braid sold me a fiddle last weekend, and I have some questions for her." Hope fluttered in Jaime's chest.

"That sounds like Laurie. She's in the back. I'll let her know you're here." The woman bounced through a door behind her.

Jaime took in all the antiques surrounding them. Last

time she was there, she thought everything was charming. This time, she wondered how many pieces had ghosts attached to them.

"I'm ready for this nightmare to be over." Drew released her hand and leaned on the counter. He looked as exhausted as Jaime felt.

"You and me both." But then what? Go on like nothing ever happened? Keep casually dating? What if Ella got attached to him? What if Jaime was the one getting attached? Jaime shoved those thoughts away. She didn't have time to dwell on her insecurities.

The door groaned open, and Laurie walked to the counter. She wore her brown hair in its long braid once again. Her brown eyes sparkled as she rested her arms on the counter. "I remember you. How is the fiddle?"

Jaime straightened her shoulders. "Well, it looked great over the couch, but you forgot to mention something in your sales pitch. I think you forgot to tell us it was haunted."

The mirth disappeared from Laurie's tanned face. "Haunted." It was a statement, not a question.

"Yes, haunted." *No matter how crazy it sounds, Jaime, stick to your guns*, she thought.

Laurie's gaze flicked from Jaime to Drew. "Do you also believe it's haunted?"

Drew nodded. "I know it is. But I don't know why or how to make the ghosts move on." He placed a business card on the counter. "I'm with Restless Spirits, Incorporated, located up the street."

"I know that place. You guys helped a friend of mine get rid of a ghost in her house last summer." Laurie sighed as she lifted the card. "Come on back." She opened the pass through at the end of the counter and ushered Jaime and Drew behind it. She led them through the door and into her back office. Objects cluttered the room like the antiques did at the front of the store, with books and papers all over the small, wooden desk and the creaky wooden floor. She moved a stack of papers off an antique chaise lounge along the right wall. "Please sit down."

Jaime and Drew lowered themselves onto the seat. The cushion didn't give much under Jaime's weight. Laurie grabbed the chair from behind her desk and dragged it over to them.

She sat, running her fingers through her hair. "I take it you've seen the ghost and the shadow?"

Jaime blinked. This woman believed them? Without questioning them? She arrived prepared to argue her case, but the whole conversation took a turn. She squirmed on the seat.

"Yes. We have. The ghost talked to my daughter."

"And the shadow tried to kill me a couple of times," Drew added.

Laurie pressed her full lips together. "I'm sorry. I've seen them both, too. But I thought they were gone when I hadn't seen them in a while. I thought it was safe to sell the fiddle."

"So, you knew?" Jaime didn't hide the surprise in her voice. "Why didn't you tell us?"

"Most people don't believe in ghosts, and I guess I wanted the sale." She crossed her legs. "That's a terrible excuse."

"How much do you know about the fiddle? I remember you said it belonged to a pair of star-crossed lovers." Drew rested his forearms on his legs.

"That's the legend the old man who sold it to me told me."

"What's the whole legend?" Jaime heard the edge in her own voice. Haunted. A legend. All things this woman could have told them to begin with.

"Yes."

Jaime fought the urge to explode. She had a daughter to protect, for crying out loud. Drew reached out and touched her arm, the gesture calming. How did he know?

"Start at the beginning," he said, his hazel eyes on the older woman.

Laurie sighed again. "According to the gentleman, a young Irish immigrant made the fiddle. Music was and still is important to people in the Blue Ridge Mountains, but it especially lifted their spirits when they didn't have a whole lot after the turn of the twentieth century."

Jaime perked up, the history geek inside her soaking in the words. "Several families actually went from North Carolina to Virginia and back again looking for work on different farms."

Laurie nodded. "That's right. The Irishman was like that, migrating from one farm to the next, and music helped brighten a long work day. He played his fiddle almost every night.

"Then one night at a church gathering, his playing caught the attention of a young woman. They started talking, and one thing led to another. By the end of the night, The Irishman wanted to court her."

Jaime smiled at the old-fashioned word. Courting always made things sound more serious than dating did. She pictured the redhead from her dream approaching the young man. She imagined Melinda started the conversation without giving it a second thought, and the Irishman tumbled head over heels in that moment.

"How did the fiddle get cursed?" Drew scooted forward, his right knee bobbing up and down.

Laurie held up a hand. "I'm getting there. See, the woman's family was more well-to-do than the Irishman. Her father didn't like the idea of her marrying some poor farmer, and he forbade it.

"The Irishman didn't take no for an answer. He played his fiddle at her window, waiting for her to come out. Her father came instead. He broke the young man's bow in half and told him to get off his property.

"The young woman bought her love a new bow because she didn't want her father running her life. When it was ready, she snuck out of the house and found her way to a secret meeting spot they had in the mountains. She gave him the bow, and they made plans to run away together."

"I think I know where this story is going. They didn't make it." Jaime's heart hurt for the two star-crossed lovers.

"They did not. Legend has it the young woman's father made a deal with the devil to find the lovers and stop them. The devil was all too eager for the bargain and gave the greedy man the power to do it. In a rage, the woman's father found the lovers and killed the Irishman. He fell on the fiddle, his blood soaking into it. The woman, heartbroken and angry, grabbed her father's shotgun. She shot him on the spot. His blood mingled with the young man's.

"After both were buried, the young woman started seeing the Irishman's ghost, but he wasn't alone. They say when the devil came to collect, he bound both of their spirits and cursed the fiddle."

"The shadow," Drew interrupted. "That shadow is her father, isn't he?"

"It makes sense," Jaime agreed.

"So, how do we break the curse?" Both of Drew's knees bounced.

"Wait, how did we unlock the curse?" Jaime settled a hand on one of his knees to steady it.

Laurie tossed her braid over her shoulder and tapped her nails on her desk. "If you'll let me finish."

Drew cleared his throat. "Sorry. Go on."

"Please," Jaime added.

The older lady pressed her lips together and waited for her small audience's full attention. Satisfied that she had it, she continued. "Now, where was I? Oh, yes. The young woman discovered she was pregnant soon after her young man and her father died. After she gave birth to her son, she noticed that every time her bow was near the fiddle, which she couldn't bear to part with, the shadow would appear. Many times it tried to hurt her son. She made the hard decision to bury the fiddle and the bow in two separate places. They say she died of a broken heart several years later." She sat back in her chair, a pleased expression on her face.

"That's it?" Drew asked, disappointment lacing his voice. "No revelations on how we got cursed or on how to break it?"

"I don't know. The old man never told me, but I've seen the ghost and the shadow in the store. They never bothered me, though." Laurie uncrossed her legs. "Come to think of it, the old man said they never bothered him, either."

"How much of that story is true?" Jaime wondered aloud. The story sounded like nothing but a legend.

"Again, I don't know to be honest." Laurie shrugged. "That's the story that came with the fiddle. I wish I had more to tell you."

"Still doesn't explain how we can stop it." Drew climbed to his feet and walked around his chair. He pressed his hand on the top of the back. His fingers dug into the worn fabric.

"Wait." Jaime thought about the story, picking the words apart piece by piece. She remembered what Drew had told her about Tristan's visions. A pretty woman, probably Melinda. The man shooting him, Melinda's father. The fiddle and the bow buried separately. "He's looking for his treasure," she muttered.

"What?" She noticed Drew watched her.

Ignoring him, she pulled Ella's drawing of the long, skinny, brown box out of her bag. She tapped the sheet as it all clicked into place. "Jeremiah is searching for the bow." She met Drew's eyes. "I think we have to find it."

Laurie chuckled. "Sounds plausible to me. One set of lovers has to free another set of lovers from the dark. Sounds poetic."

Jaime's cheeks heated. "Oh, we're not..."

"Nothing's official." Drew's face glowed bright red.

Laurie arched a brow. "Sure. I've been around long enough to see two people who like each other. You're not fooling anybody."

"Where did you buy the fiddle, by the way?" Jaime asked.

"Oh, found it in an old barn on the outskirts of Asheville. The man said he found it in a dump down in Raleigh."

"My uncle lived in Raleigh." Drew's face paled, the earlier blushing gone.

Laurie climbed to her feet. "Well, I wish you luck. That's all I know."

Jaime stood and shook the older woman's hand. "Thank you for telling us the legend. I think it's given us somewhere to start."

"You're welcome. If the curse is true, I hope you can break it."

If Jaime's suggestion panned out, all they had to do was find a bow buried somewhere in the Blue Ridge Mountains. No big deal. Drew sighed as he and Jaime walked out of the antique store. He dreaded the idea of searching for the mysterious box. He thought of how many miles the mountains covered in North Carolina alone.

"You know, she didn't really give us much." He shoved his cold hands into his coat pockets.

"She gave us the bow, and my dream gave us the names." Jaime jogged to keep up with him.

"But we don't have the first clue of where to look." Drew stopped walking as he tossed his hands into the air, letting all of his frustration out. "That bow could be buried anywhere."

"Well, we have a pretty good idea that you're related to the star-crossed lovers, so we'll start there." Jaime bumped his hip. "Jeremiah came here from Ireland. Where did you grow up?"

"Boone, but that doesn't mean anything."

"What about your dad?"

He narrowed his eyes as he thought about her question. "I

want to say Boone also? But I don't know. He met my mom in Charlotte."

"Your grandfather?"

"No clue." Drew shrugged. "I didn't know that side of the family well."

"Okay." Jaime strode past him and led the way to the car, her head held high. "We start with Boone and go from there. Melinda was also a Beauchamp, and according to the legend, she came from money. We can research her as well." She placed her hands on the roof of the car. "We're not totally at a loss."

"I guess." Drew doubted Jaime's idea as he slid into the car.

During the next couple of days, Jaime kept busy with school and taking Ella to practice with McKenna. Digging into the Keane family tree hovered low on her list of priorities. Sticking to her routine helped her deal with the newfound strangeness in her life.

Drew focused on the one thing in his life he controlled, his ghost disruptor. He sat in the middle of his living room floor, electronic pieces spread out around him. He broke the ghost disruptor down into its smallest components. It worked. His baby worked. But it kept taking out all the other electronic equipment and then overheating. He needed something that remained more stable than his current configuration. Focusing on his machine blocked him from worrying about the curse and how far the shadow might be able to reach him.

Since he'd been working from home, he hadn't seen the shadow once. Aaron said that the shadow didn't show at the office, either. His boss expressed regret at leaving the fiddle out in the alley a few days earlier. The salt had confined the spirit, but the wind blew a gap in the circle. That was how the shadow left its prison and attacked Drew in his office. Aaron kept the instrument in his office closet for the time being, a thicker circle of salt around it.

Aaron grunted when Drew asked him not to burn the fiddle. He came around when Drew explained how he and Jaime wanted to end the curse. He listened, asked a few questions, and in the end, respected the decision.

Drew flipped through the research on his laptop. Ideas and half-baked plans flicked past. He kept coming back to a website that sold a Klystron emitter. It was the science behind microwaves, and Drew thought it might disrupt a ghost without disrupting everything else, and maybe not overheat in the process. He loved the idea, but his heart sank when he saw the price tag. Seventy thousand dollars priced too rich for his blood, and Restless Spirits didn't have that kind of money in its spending budget.

However, he would bet anything that The Greene Institute for Paranormal Research probably did. Tabitha's family owned the place, and Aaron had cut his teeth working for them. But neither dealt with them anymore. He thought about asking Tabitha, but he hadn't worked up the nerve yet.

Eventually, he moved over to some of his favorite research websites. He hoped someone might offer another, cheaper idea.

A knock on the door interrupted his train of thought. Groaning, Drew stood and answered it. Someone shoved a bag of McDonald's breakfast food into his face. The smell of hot, rich bacon filled his nose.

"I thought you'd be here." Tristan pushed the warm bag into Drew's hand as he walked into the tiny basement apartment. "You've been anti-social the past couple of days."

"*You're* calling *me* anti-social. Isn't that like the pot calling the kettle black?" Drew closed the door behind him. He dropped the bag onto the counter that separated the kitchen from the living room that doubled as his bedroom. It was the only surface that offered any space. He had yet to shove his bed back into the couch. "What are you doing here, man? Aren't you supposed to be in class?" He took out one of the biscuits. "Aren't you teaching a class?"

Tristan grabbed the other sandwich. "It's Saturday. Did you forget what day it is?" He unwrapped his bacon, egg, and cheese biscuit and inhaled a large bite. "And McKenna sent me."

Drew unwrapped his own biscuit and tiptoed across the parts-filled floor to his bed. It squeaked when he sat down. "Just because I haven't talked to anybody lately doesn't mean you need to check on me." He raised the biscuit. "But thank you." He bit in. "This Mac's idea, too?"

"Nah. I figured you probably hadn't eaten anything." Tristan cleaned off a ratty brown armchair and sat down. He removed some bacon from the biscuit and tossed it into his mouth. "McKenna filled me in yesterday on the attack. How are you?"

"Good." He gestured to the floor. "Busy."

"What is all this stuff?" Tristan leaned forward, studying the pieces on the floor.

"The disruptor. I'm trying to make improvements." Drew collected the parts and tossed them into a black garbage bag.

"Have you?"

"I have a few ideas, but they're expensive." Drew sighed, dropping onto the bed with his sausage biscuit in one hand. "What did Mac tell you?"

"Every bit of it." Tristan polished off the biscuit. "So, it's your turn to have a ghost attack you, and I have to hear about it from my girlfriend? What gives?"

"Well, you saw the first attack." Drew talked around a full mouth.

"Yeah, but McKenna had to tell me about the second." Tristan punched him on the arm. Drew winced, not expecting it to be so hard. "You're supposed to be my best friend, and I've lost one too many friends to a ghost."

Drew winced again, this time at the guilt. Zack had been Tristan's best friend, too. "Sorry, man. You're right." He set his half-eaten biscuit in the wrapper on a nearby side table. "Maybe you can help." He held out his hand. "Where is my family from?"

Tristan studied his hand before meeting his eyes. "What?"

Drew shook his hand at him. "Come on, you can see the past, right?"

"That's…not how it works. You know that's not how it works."

Drew dropped his hand, feeling like an idiot. "Yeah, I know." He jumped up, the urge to move racing through him. "I just want to know how to end this curse, that's all. Jaime's kept me up to date on any little bit of research she's found, but she didn't turn up much. I know most of my family is from the Boone area, but that still doesn't tell us where the bow is." He paced around the tiny studio apartment.

"I get it. Getting rid of Lily wasn't easy, either."

Drew paused. "Jaime's been dreaming about my great-great grandmother."

Tristan scooted to the edge of the chair. "Really? I didn't know she was psychic."

"She's not. And Jeremiah is still haunting her daughter." He blew out a breath. "Somehow, my curse dragged them in, too. I need to stop it to protect them."

"You really care about her, don't you?"

Drew nodded. "I do. Jaime and Ella. I can't let anything happen to them."

"You won't, man."

A hesitant knock interrupted them. Drew exchanged a look with Tristan. He didn't expect anyone at his door. To be fair, Tristan had arrived out of the blue. He crossed to the door and peered through the peephole. Heat flushed his cheeks as his back stiffened.

His father stood on the other side.

For a split second, Drew wanted to pretend like he wasn't home. How had his dad found him? But after a second series of knocks, Drew gave in and opened the door.

"Dad, what a pleasant surprise." He said through his teeth.

Darren Keane occupied the doorway, his hands stuffed in his coat pockets. He lifted his head, his greenish hazel eyes uncertain but clear. He ran a hand through his blond and grey short hair as he regarded his son.

"Your mother told me where you lived. She asked me to come by." The words came out coherent, no hint of slurring. All signs pointed to him being sober.

Drew didn't trust it, though. He hadn't seen his father in a long time, but he stayed wary around the man. He knew how mean Darren became when he drank. Drew stood still, gripping the doorknob so hard it began to hurt. He debated whether or not to let his father in.

Darren took a step forward, offering his hand. "I've been sober for almost a year now. Haven't touched one drink."

Drew didn't move. "Good for you."

He remembered his dad as larger than life with a bellowing voice to match. The man in front of him was the same height with a slimmer frame. Deep lines covered his face, matching the gray in his hair.

"It's good to see you, son." Darren shuffled from foot to foot.

Drew stepped back. "What do you want, Dad?" All the things he wanted to say to his father bubbled underneath the surface. Where had he been? Why didn't he sober up all those years ago? If he was sober now, why didn't he visit Drew in the hospital back in September? But he realized he didn't want the answers. He wanted his dad gone.

"I guess I'd better get going." Tristan slid past the father and son. "Promised McKenna I'd take her out to lunch."

Drew glared at his best friend. *What a traitor!* As soon as Tristan left, Drew reached a decision. He might as well get it over with. He gestured his dad into his space. It didn't feel right having him there, and he plotted about talking to his mom after this.

"Your mom told me about the fiddle, and the curse." Darren shoved his hands into his pockets again. "I was hoping you wouldn't have to face it."

Drew's fists tightened as he closed the door. He resisted the urge to slam it. "What are you talking about, Dad?"

He wanted to tell his father to go, but he swore he heard his mother's voice in the back of his mind. *"At least hear him out."* His mother's voice won. He showed his father to the chair Tristan vacated. Drew stayed standing, wanting to be taller than his father in case he needed to be on guard. He towered over Darren, but the nervous little boy inside of him wouldn't go away.

Darren sat on the edge of the chair while he shrugged out of his coat. "Your mom said you're a paranormal investigator now. You always did like that weird stuff." For once, his tone sounded sincere instead of judgmental. He draped his coat on the arm of the chair.

"Yeah. I actually make a good living doing it." Drew kept a few feet between them at all times, instinct kicking in. He crossed his arms. "Dad, what are you doing here?" He didn't want to spend time filling his dad in on every last detail of his life. He didn't think the man cared anyway.

"I told you." Darren pulled an old, wooden box out of a

reusable grocery bag. A bag Drew hadn't noticed him carrying. "It's about the fiddle."

"What do you know about the fiddle?"

His father sighed. "It's part of the Keane Family Curse. Something I should have warned you about a long time ago."

Every muscle in Drew's body tensed. He learned from the conversation with his mom that his dad probably knew about the fiddle and the ghosts, but to hear him come out and say it floored Drew. It made the curse worse somehow.

"You knew there was a possibility some shadow thing would try to kill me?" Drew fought to keep his voice even. He eyed the closest wall, wishing he could punch it.

"Son." Darren rested his arms on his knees. "I didn't know the shadow would target you. I thought you'd never come near the fiddle." He groaned. "I didn't even really believe the legend."

"You mean, the one about the star-crossed lovers and the father who made a deal with the devil? Yeah, I've heard it already." Drew accepted the need to move again. He stalked around the small space.

"You see how crazy it sounds, right? But I guess in your line of work it isn't that crazy after all." Darren rubbed the back of his neck. Drew froze when he saw the gesture, a move he did way too often when he felt nervous or unsure. He didn't want to acknowledge that he shared anything in common with the man.

Darren waited a beat before continuing. "How did you find it?"

"My girlfriend bought it at an antique store."

"I see." His dad made space on a nearby table and set the wooden box there. "Should've known it would find you. It always finds at least one of us every generation. That shadow, whether or not it's the man from the story, killed my brother."

Drew softened. "Mom mentioned seeing the fiddle in his house before he died."

"It also killed two of your great-uncles. I didn't believe that story when your grandpa told me after your uncle Charlie died, but I do now. Your mom and I tried to throw it away." He hung his head. "Your mom did. I wouldn't touch it." He looked up. "Let me ask you something. Did you ever get blood on the fiddle?"

"Yes." He remembered the night in Jaime's living room. The fiddle called to him even then, and he nicked his finger when he touched it. He hadn't given that moment a second thought. "What does that have to do with anything?"

"Keane blood kicks off the curse."

Drew dropped onto his squeaky bed. The curse didn't choose him at random. The curse *belonged* to him. No wonder all signs pointed to his family. His heart sank. He placed Jaime and Ella in danger, and he didn't know how to protect them.

"How do I break it? Why hasn't anyone else broken it yet?" Drew wiped his face with both hands, his legs bouncing.

"Because no one knew how. All the ghost ever asks for is his treasure, but he never said what it was. And the shadow kills quickly after that." Darren gave a half grin. "I'm proud you've lasted this long."

Drew eyed his father. "I do this for a living, remember. I deal with this stuff all the time." He didn't want to believe any of this. As far as he knew, his father was drunk and rambling again—only his dad spoke clearly. He sounded sober and clear-headed, and he hadn't taken a drink from a bottle once. And, Drew had tangled with the shadow twice already.

"No one knows how to stop this thing?" He paused as a thought occurred to him. "Who or what cursed it to begin with? I've met real psychics, but no witches. As far as I know, no one can curse objects."

"I don't know, son." His father stood and stretched. "But these might hold an answer." He tapped the top of the wooden box.

"What's inside?"

Darren lifted the lid to reveal several old, yellowed envelopes. "Love letters between your great-great-grandparents and letters your great-great-grandma wrote to her son before he was born. Your great-grandpa. Your grandpa held onto these with an iron grip." His fingers grazed the edge of one of the letters. "I've only read a few of these myself, but I'm hoping she left a clue about how to end this."

Drew narrowed his eyes. "You could be making all of this up. Maybe building up to ask me for money?" He knew he said too much the minute the words tumbled out of his mouth. He wished he could suck them back in.

Darren's expression grew hard. He shoved his hands into his coat pockets. "I'm not here for money. In fact, I haven't touched a drink in a year. I told you that when I walked in." He zipped his coat with a flick of his wrist. "I came here because I realized I should have told you all of this a long time ago. I was a shit father to you and your sister. And this probably won't make up for any of it, but it's a start. I don't want to lose my son the same way I lost my brother." He swallowed as he stormed to the door.

Drew wanted nothing more than to sink into the floor. He cleared his throat. "Thank you. For telling me." He lifted his head. "Do you want to help me end this?"

"I can't." Darren shook his head. "The one who activates the curse is the one who has to stop it. That's the number one thing your grandpa told me." He met his son's eyes. "It looks like you're the one. But if I remember anything else your grandpa told me, I'll let you know."

"Thank you." Drew stood and wiped his palms on his jeans, unsure of how to react to this new version of his dad. Did they hug? Shake hands? In the end, Darren chose for him. He relaxed his shoulders, waved, and walked out, the front door closing in his wake.

16

Tears burned at the corners of Drew's eyes. He brushed them, determined not to let any of them fall. He had already shed too many tears over his father growing up. It wasn't the time to let that happen. He had a curse to break.

He reached for the bag with all of his disruptor parts, but stopped on the plain and simple wooden box, no ornamentation on it anywhere. Drew plucked out the first letter and eased it open. The yellowing paper displayed tears and rips around the edges and gave off a musty smell. The handwriting offered no flourish to it whatsoever, but the writer drew each letter neat and straight. Drew glanced at the signature. "Le grá, Jeremiah." He sank onto his bed and began to read.

Mo grá,

Not seeing you these past two weeks is breaking my heart. I miss you. I know you're trying, and your da won't let us be together, but everything feels empty. Your sister is a dear for carrying these letters back and forth. I've told her thank you, but I don't feel like that is enough.

I miss your rose-colored hair, your sparkling green eyes, your laugh, your smile. Look at me going on. My brothers back in Dublin would have a laugh at all of these pretty words. But I mean every one of them. From the moment we met, you're all I can think about.

I don't know why your da hates me so. I've been nothing but nice to him. I know I don't have fancy clothes or a fancy horse, but I'd love you every day for the rest of our lives.

Please find a way to talk your da into letting you come to town, or maybe go for a walk in the woods. We can meet in our special spot, and no one will ever know. I've never told anyone about that spot, and I'll take the secret to my grave.

I await your next letter.

Le grá,

Jeremiah

"Wow," Drew breathed. "Why didn't I inherit your game?" He folded the letter with care and tucked it back into its box.

Jaime needed to see this box and all of its contents. Maybe something in the letters would match something in one of her dreams. He pulled out his phone and texted her.

DREW: *Got something you need to see. Are you free?*

It felt like an eternity before she wrote back. The three dots danced on the screen, teasing him.

JAIME: *Ella is in the middle of a lesson with McKenna. Can we meet tonight?*

DREW: *Yeah. Text me when you get home.*

Drew thought about his great-great grandfather's signature. Even though he didn't know what it meant, he added, *Le grá, Drew.*

The three dots popped up beside Jaime's name. *Oh, no. Was that too cheesy?*

JAIME: *What does that mean?*

Drew scratched his chin. Maybe he laid it on too thick with that signature. He found an online translator and typed in the words. They were Irish for "with love." His pulse jumped. Did he just say "love" to Jaime? Shit! Were they even ready for that step? He stared at her text, trying to come up with something believable. Why did he text that? *Pull it together, Keane.* He should tell her the truth. She could look up the words just like he did. In the end, he took the coward's way.

DREW: *Nothing. See you tonight.*

He hastily put away his phone and closed the box of letters. The lid clicked shut. Grabbing the bag, he dumped all of the parts of his disruptor back onto the floor. If he planned to break the family curse, he needed something to hold back the shadow long enough for him to do it. The ghost disruptor was the answer, but it needed to work. And it needed that seventy-thousand-dollar Klystron emitter to do so. The gun shape was easy to hold. Every other part worked like clockwork. He just needed to change direction with the integral piece.

If he got this one working, maybe he could make one to keep Jaime and Ella safe until he ended the shadow.

Jaime and Ella. He knew they wanted to help, but he didn't want to put Jaime in harm's way, and he especially wanted Ella far away from this. It didn't matter that she had the ability to find things. She was ten years old. She didn't need to be anywhere near this. He bit his bottom lip as he gathered his tools. He cared about Ella as much as he did her mother, even if Ella showed her animosity toward him.

Drew turned his attention back to the bits and pieces. He still thought the Greene Institute might have the part he needed, and maybe, just maybe, they would let him have it. He needed to talk to Tabitha and Aaron about this. He didn't imagine his friends would agree right away. Whether Tabitha and Aaron helped him get the part or not, they might know something about curses. They knew more about this ghost stuff then he did. He opened a video chat on his laptop.

Aaron raised an eyebrow when he answered it. "Drew, it's Saturday. We have the weekend off. Why are you calling me?"

Tabitha slid into view, her short hair in all directions. "Hi, Drew. What's going on?"

"Good. You're both there. Well, it turns out you were right. The shadow, Jaime's ghost, and the fiddle are all connected to me." He took a deep breath and told them about his family, the possible curse, his blood dropping on the fiddle, and the conversation with his dad.

Aaron's curmudgeonly expression smoothed out while Tabitha's blue eyes grew wide.

"Have you two ever come across actual curses?" Drew finished.

"I can't say I have." Aaron turned to his wife. "Tabby?"

She nodded. "I was a teenager, following my sisters around and learning the family business. They were working on a haunting down in New Bern, an old plantation house with some of its original furniture. Apparently, it had been passed down from one family member to the next, and all of them had died on their fiftieth birthday."

"Creepy," Drew commented.

"I'll say." Aaron adjusted himself to a more comfortable position.

"Naturally, the owner was getting close to his fiftieth birthday and had started seeing the ghost of a man around his house. We investigated and learned that his ancestor had killed a man a least a hundred years before. Apparently, the murdered man came back to kill his descendants when they turned the age he was when he died."

"It always comes down to revenge, doesn't it?" Drew muttered. He peered around the empty, quiet room and wished for some company at that moment. He used to like the silence. He shivered. "What happened? Did you stop it?"

Tabitha's mouth formed a perfect line. "You know the Greene Institute isn't into actually helping people these days. They're more into the research. But in her own destructive way, my oldest sister Lisa did help this guy. I didn't agree with her methods, but it got the job done."

"Let me guess." Aaron looked at Tabitha out of the corner of his eye. "She killed the guy."

"No. He's still very much alive. She burned down the house, but he and his family were out of the house at the time. All she did was slice his hand and drop some of his blood into the flames."

"Whoa. Extreme." Drew swallowed, hoping he didn't have to burn or slice to end his family's curse. He rubbed his palm, imagining a knife cutting through it.

"Lisa never does anything halfway. She always strives to get Dad's attention, especially since Corrie is his favorite." Tabitha shrugged.

Aaron studied his wife. "I thought you were his favorite."

She snorted and nudged him. "That was before I abandoned the family business to run off with some headstrong man." She rolled her eyes as she turned her attention back to Drew. "How can we help you end your curse?"

"Well, how does one get cursed? Does it involve magic or a spell? We've come across psychics, but I don't think I've ever met a witch. Hell, I've been friends with Tristan my whole life, but I don't think he has the power to curse people." Drew picked up a nearby pen and chewed on the end of it.

Tabitha laughed. "I think if Tristan or McKenna could curse people, we'd all be in trouble." She took a deep breath.

"As far as I know, there's no research that explains it scientifically, but I have theories. Aaron, have you seen anything?"

Aaron rubbed the dark stubble on his chin. He stopped shaving a few days before, saying he was ready for his winter beard. Tabitha grunted at him, not on board with the decision. "Most of what I've read are theories. Like ghosts are the strongest energy left from a person, curses come from strong energy, too. Usually a heated moment when tensions are running high. Or a strong bout of anger at the moment of death."

"Like if someone is trying to kill you with a shotgun?" Drew asked, remembering parts of Tristan's vision and the legend. "Or does kill you?"

"I'd say so. You said both Jeremiah's blood and his girlfriend's father's blood landed on the fiddle in the story?" Aaron's brown eyes became serious.

"Yeah."

"Her father could have cursed the fiddle with his dying breath," Tabitha suggested. "Or his hatred for Jeremiah was so strong that it tied both of their spirits to the instrument. I don't think he actually made a deal with the devil."

"Okay, so no witches." Drew drummed his fingers on his desk.

"I can honestly say I've never met one," Tabitha said.

"Nor the devil?"

Aaron cocked his head to the side. "I wouldn't go that far, but I don't think he's involved with this."

"So, to end the curse, we may be looking at blood and fire once we find Jeremiah's treasure, which might be this bow."

"Possibly if your dad believes your blood started this whole thing." Aaron sipped from a coffee mug that read "World's Greatest Genius."

Drew shifted in his seat, ready to dive into the other reason he called them. "This is going to sound weird."

"You've asked a lot of weird questions since we started working together. Out with it." Aaron reached into his back pocket and cursed. "Man, what I would kill for a cigarette."

Tabitha patted his arm. "You're doing good, babe."

He growled in response.

"Anyway." Drew jumped in before Aaron pegged him as the sacrifice to the cigarette gods. "I've been tweaking the ghost disruptor, and I think I've found a way to make it work."

"You're still messing with that thing?" Aaron sat back on his couch.

"I still think it's a great idea," Tabitha said. She leaned in, resting her chin in her hand.

"It keeps taking out all my equipment," Aaron grumbled.

Drew snapped his fingers. "Exactly. But I've found a different way to disrupt a ghost's energy using Klystron emitters."

Aaron raised a brow.

"Go on," Tabitha said as she bit into a cookie.

"It's the technology that makes microwaves work." Drew started talking faster as his excitement built. "The microwaves can mess up a ghost's energy field. If I could put together a series of op-amps with the emitter at the end of the circuit, it just might work."

"I don't understand any of that, but you've got my support," Aaron announced.

Tabitha mimed a finger gun. "We'd have our own ghost blaster. No proton pack required."

"But there's a problem." All of his earlier excitement died at the thought of breaking the news to Aaron and Tabitha. "A Klystron emitter costs seventy thousand dollars."

Aaron spit coffee all over his lap. "What?"

"We can't afford it," Drew said.

Tabitha tapped her chin. "I bet the Greene Institute has

one. Lisa is always dropping money on anything she thinks will give her an advantage."

Drew winced. He hated asking his next question. "Do you think they'd let me use one or look at blueprints to try and build my own?"

Tabitha laughed again. "Lisa sharing any of her tech secrets? Not a chance."

Drew's hope deflated. It looked like he would be trudging through the mountains with bags of salt. "I'm so close."

Tabitha pressed her lips together. "I'll talk to her. See what I can do."

"More importantly, when do you plan on breaking the curse? We can get the team together to help you." The screen rocked as Aaron brought his computer closer.

"No. I don't want anyone else getting hurt. I have to do this on my own."

"You're not alone, you know. We're family," Aaron insisted.

"I know." Drew squared his shoulders. Talking to his father made one thing clear to him. "This is my family's curse, and I'm the only one who can break it."

Saturday mornings remained sacred in Ella's mind. She loved to spend it hanging out in pajamas and watching TV while she stuffed sugary goodness into her mouths. With no school, Ella thought of it as the laziest day of the week. But McKenna decided to ignore all of the rules and make Ella practice on Saturday morning.

Never mind the fact they had practiced for the past two days, and the vision refused to pop back into her mind. She tried, too.

Meanwhile, Ella aced every other test McKenna threw at her. Hidden keys in the conference room? Found them in, like, five seconds. Hidden mug in McKenna's desk? Easy as pie. A small earring stuffed in the back of a drawer? No challenge at all. But trying to find objects outside of the office posed a problem.

After the third failed attempt at locating a book hidden outside in her mom's car, Ella dropped into a leather conference room chair. "It's not working."

"It's okay, honey. You're doing great!" Mom beamed.

"No, I'm not." Ella tossed her hands into the air. "I suck at this."

"Not true." McKenna sat down next to her. "You found everything else."

"Yeah, everything in this office. I always find stuff when I'm in the same building, but it doesn't work if something is *outside* the building." Ella wrinkled her nose when she heard the whine in her own voice. She folded her arms on the table and lowered her forehead to them. "I can't do it."

Someone rubbed her back. "Yes, you can."

Ella kept her eyes on her shoes. "You're supposed to say that. You're my mom."

McKenna cleared her throat. "Jaime, I have an idea. One I wanted to try earlier, but I wasn't sure how you'd feel about it."

"Okay." Mom sounded wary.

"It might be dangerous."

Ella's head snapped up, the idea of danger catching her attention. "How dangerous?"

McKenna sighed. "I know you know the fiddle is in the building."

"Oh, yeah. That thing's been buzzing since I first walked in here." Ella rested her chin in her hand.

McKenna glanced from Ella to her mom and back again. She kept her hand steady on Ella's back. "What if we tried working in the room with the fiddle? The salt circle is still around it. The shadow is contained."

"It didn't hold the ghost," Mom said.

"Something I'm still researching." Mom shared the story of the ghost, Jeremiah, still being in the house and how he seemed stronger with McKenna. He hadn't come back in the last few days, but Ella felt like he kept an eye on her. Not in a creepy way, but in a "I'll keep you safe" kind of way. Even though he initially scared her, she liked having him around.

He hovered around the house, though. He either couldn't or wouldn't follow her outside of it.

McKenna suggested that maybe he latched onto Ella because of her power, but she didn't offer any proof.

"Anyway," McKenna continued. "Aaron keeps it in the closet in his office."

Mom wrinkled her brow like she did when she was getting ready to say no, but she didn't really want to. "I don't know about this."

"We won't open the closet door." McKenna lifted a hand, palm out. "But I was thinking, maybe Jeremiah triggered the vision, and since he was part of the fiddle, the fiddle might do the same."

Mom sighed as she sat down. "It's a good theory, but Ella shouldn't be able to do that at all. Outside of that one vision, she hasn't had visions of other objects. She didn't locate the book."

"True, but it might be a part of her power that might grow in time."

"What do you mean?" Ella piped up. Her stomach did a somersault. "You mean when I get to be your age, objects will just pop into my head." She swallowed, the whole idea terrifying her. "I don't think I want that." She gripped the edge of the table with her sweaty hands.

"I don't know how your power will progress. It's just a theory, that's all. If I have your permission, I can tell Tristan, and maybe we can see if something like this is in his grandfather's journals."

Ella went still. Telling more people about her power? She shot a look at her mom, her whole body screaming *NO*. McKenna was one thing, but Tristan seemed so cool and kind of cute in an old guy way. She definitely didn't want him to think she was a freak.

"It's okay," McKenna soothed. "I know how you're feeling, remember? And Tristan is like us."

"What?"

"It's true," Mom said. "Tristan has his own psychic power. He can see the history of a person or a place."

Ella chewed her bottom lip. "So he won't think I'm weird?"

"Oh, of course not!" McKenna smiled. "He worries other people will think he's weird."

Ella shifted in her seat. "Well, in that case, I guess it's okay."

"In the meantime, do you want to try near the fiddle?" McKenna directed the question to her. Not her mom, but her, treating her like an adult old enough to make her own decisions. Ella sneaked a glance at her mom.

"It's your choice."

"Okay." Ella nodded.

The evil, monotonous buzz increased as Ella and her mom followed McKenna into Aaron's office. It was the second biggest room in the whole place, not counting the open space where McKenna's desk sat. Windows with drawn blinds covered one wall. The other three walls were plain white with a few framed posters of comic book characters on them. A dark, wooden desk with a big, black leather chair behind it occupied the middle of the room. Two small plastic chairs rested in front of the desk. She noticed the closet in the back right corner. Ella swore she not only heard the buzz, but felt heat coming off the door.

She perched on the edge of the desk while her mom took one of the plastic chairs. McKenna stood next to Ella.

"You ready to try again?"

Ella cast a wary glance to the closet door and took a deep breath. She had to act brave, not like a scared, little kid.

"Yeah."

"Okay, just like we practiced. Close your eyes and relax. Think about the wooden box and the sound it made."

Ella saw the dark back of her own eyelids while the fiddle's buzzing rang in her ears. She focused on it, unable to block it out. She waited and waited, but nothing happened. She wanted to give up, but then she heard that soft, mournful melody. The same one she heard in her bedroom.

Her hand landed on someone's arm. "I hear it."

"I've got you." Mom. It was Mom's arm.

The image of the wooden box snapped into focus. Darkness still surrounded it, but this time, everything focused sharper and clearer. "I see rocks and dirt," Ella said. "I think the box is underground."

"Can you hear anything? Smell? Touch? Anything other than see?"

Ella hadn't tried that before. The last time she saw the vision, it scared her to death. But this time, she stayed calm, like McKenna did when she read emotions. She could do this. She tried to listen past the object's musical vibration. Were there any other sounds? "I hear a whoosh noise."

"Whoosh?" Mom asked.

"Yeah. It's like whooooooosssshhhh." She drew the sound out and made it continuous. "Kind of like when you run a bath, but harder?"

"Running water?" McKenna guessed.

"Yeah. Yeah."

She reached out, but couldn't touch anything, and she didn't smell anything, either. She squeezed her eyes to shut them tighter, trying to find any other details. She thought she latched onto something when a door rattled. Ella's eyes snapped open. The closet door shook like someone fought to get out.

Mom grabbed Ella and yanked her off the desk.

"Let's get out of here." McKenna followed them out of the

room, shutting the door behind her. The noise stopped as quickly as it started.

"What was that?" Mom asked.

McKenna stared at the office door. "The shadow knows that you're looking for the bow. I think he's trying to stop you." She met Ella's eyes. "But he can't get out of the salt circle."

Ella gripped her mom's arm. "You promise?"

"I promise."

A s they stepped out into the rainy afternoon, Jaime held on to her daughter. "You know I think you and your power are amazing, right?"

"Mom!" Ella ducked her head. "It's okay."

"It's more than okay." Jaime angled away enough to look down at Ella. "It's amazing. Because of you, we know the bow is in a box and buried somewhere near a waterfall."

"Yeah, but I don't know where that waterfall is." Ella squirmed out of Jaime's hold and yanked her hood over her head. "Jeremiah is going to be stuck in our house forever, and that shadow thing is going to be stuck in that office forever." Shoving her hands into her pockets, she hunched her shoulders.

Jaime popped open her umbrella. "With your power and my research skills, we're going to help Drew break that curse." She nudged her daughter with a hip. "The three of us make a good team."

Ella didn't answer. Instead, she scrunched down further as she stomped in every puddle on the sidewalk.

"Is everything okay?" Jaime asked after a tense silence settled between them.

"Yeah," Ella bit out.

"Drew texted me while you were working with McKenna. He said he wanted to show us something before you go to Kelly's to spend the night. He said it's pretty cool."

"So." Ella kicked a small rock. Her mood seemed to plummet the minute Jaime mentioned Drew.

"El?"

Ella whirled, tossing her hands in the air. "Leave me alone. You and Drew go do your whole grown-up thing and leave me out. Like always."

The rain poured down with heavy, fat drops, but Jaime stopped walking. "Where did that come from?"

"Just forget it."

"Ella, talk to me."

Anger flashed in Ella's dark eyes. "You don't talk to me." She took off, racing up the sidewalk.

Jaime groaned. Normally, she'd give Ella time, but not alone on the streets of downtown Asheville. Her hand firmly gripped on the umbrella handle, she ran after Ella. Cold rain pelted her arms as she darted up the sidewalk. Her longer legs ate the distance, and she caught Ella in a matter of moments. Plus, she didn't need to dash around too many people.

"Ella." She rested a hand on the young girl's shoulder and steered her under an awning. She then walked around to face her. "What's going on?"

Tears streaked down Ella's face, mingling with the rain already on her cheeks. "Nothing."

"Ella, you were amazing today. Why the sudden change?"

"You're always hanging out with him." Her finger jabbed in the direction of the Restless Spirits office.

"Drew? Is he the problem?" Jaime rubbed her daughter's shoulders. She realized that Ella had grown in the last few weeks. The top of her head came to Jaime's chest.

"Yeah." Ella's shoulders slumped. "No. I don't know."

"Tell me what you do know. Why are you upset? Are you mad because Drew is hanging around more often?"

"Kind of. Ever since this whole ghost thing started, it's like he practically lives with us." The anger vanished, leaving a sad and scared girl behind. She fell into her mom's arms. "You don't have time for me anymore."

"What?" Jaime held on tightly, rubbing Ella's back. "I always have time for you, no matter what."

"Not now. You always made me stay with Layne last week." Ella sniffled. "I want to stay with you."

"Oh, baby." Jaime wanted to argue, but she realized Ella was right. In trying to keep her safe, she pushed her away. "I'm sorry. I'm so sorry. I was trying to keep you away from the ghosts, not trying to keep you away from me. Nor trying to replace you with Drew." She thought the idea came across as crazy, but she didn't voice that opinion.

Ella stepped back. Jaime tucked a strand of hair behind her daughter's ear. "I would never push you away. Ever. You're the best thing in my life."

"Even better than Drew?"

"Yes, of course." Jaime chuckled. "I like Drew a lot, but if it came down to you or him, you'd win every time. And Ella, I think he knows that." She blocked the tears threatening in her own eyes, hoping they wouldn't fall. "But, Ella, I'd like him to be around more often. Is that okay?"

Ella shrugged. "I guess."

"I promise when this is over, we'll do something together. Just the two of us. No Drew. No Layne. You have my word."

"You promise?"

"I promise. Now, let's head to the car before the rain gets worse and we're soaking wet." She stood and held out her hand. Ella took it, even though she argued she was too old to hold her mother's hand. "You know, you're ditching me for Kelly tonight."

Ella turned her face to the fat drops of rain and seemed to think that over. "True, but I promise she won't replace you."

"Good."

Together, they made their way to the car in the pouring rain.

With love?" Jaime asked as she ushered Drew inside.

"What?" Color rose in Drew's cheeks. She loved making him blush.

"With love. You texted that to me today. I looked up the meaning of *le grá*." All through the day, Jaime held on to those two words. She realized neither one of them had said the L-word yet. She marveled that Drew declared it first. Before she read those words, she didn't know how much she needed to hear them. "Did you mean it?" She raised a hand, her pulse jumping. "Wait. I'm not sure if I want to know."

Drew laced his fingers through hers, lowering her hand. "I've thought about it all day, and yeah, I meant it."

Jaime's cheeks warmed with pleasure. How ridiculous! She wasn't a teenager anymore. "We hardly know each other."

"No, we don't." Drew inched closer. "We've been dating for almost two months."

"Seeing each other, off and on. Nothing steady." She flattened her free hand on his chest, creating space between them.

Drew's mouth curved into a mischievous smile. "Then why do you care what I texted you?"

Jaime swallowed. He made an excellent point, but she refused to acknowledge it. She cleared her throat as she pulled her hand out of his and moved out of his embrace. "So, you said you had something important to show me."

"I do." The grin stayed in place as Drew walked into the kitchen and set the bag he carried on the table. He opened it, retrieving a wooden box with a careful hand. "Jaime, these are my great-great grandparents' letters."

Jaime studied the medium-sized wooden box resting in the middle of her kitchen table. Giddiness bubbled inside her as she glanced from the box to Drew and back again. She touched the smooth, cool top like it was a sacred object.

"Have you opened it yet?" Her voice registered a notch above a whisper. She worried about any loud noise disturbing the historic treasures inside.

"Yeah. I couldn't help it. I read one letter." Drew patted the box.

"Without me?" She ran her fingers across the side. "I guess I don't blame you." How could anyone own this kind of connection to the past and not want to read every last word? She locked eyes with him. "Can I open it?"

He waved a hand. "Go for it."

The lid creaked as she lifted it. Her breath caught when she saw the wooden inside as well. Yellowing letters filled the box. A couple of them toppled over and fell to the table. Jaime wrapped her arms around the area, creating a barrier so they wouldn't continue their journey to the floor.

"Oh, wow." Her giddiness was about to bubble over like the letters. "Your great-great grandparents had so much to say."

Jaime plucked a letter from the top of the pile, taking care not to rip it and slid into the nearest chair. Drew sat next her, resting an arm across the back of her chair.

The light and delicate penmanship flourished across the page. The writer misspelled a few words, and some mountain colloquialisms peppered the letter. She swore she heard Melinda's slow, Southern rhythm. So different from her grandmother's speech, still thick with the accent of the small Chinese village where she grew up. She sometimes used English and Chinese interchangeably. Jaime couldn't speak Chinese fluently, but her grandmother always wanted her to have a connection.

She wished she had a tangible connection like Drew's letters to the ancestors who left their homeland and made a new life in America. They were journeys filled with hardship and struggles, especially when they couldn't speak the language.

Jaime cleared her throat and begin to read:

My Love,

Our child grows more and more inside me each day. It's getting harder to keep this secret. I think Mama suspects. She watches me like a hawk these days.

I wish you would come back for us. I'm ready to be your wife, the mother of your child. And this child will be loved. He will grow up, loving who he wants to love. You'll never be cruel or mean to him. You're never cruel to me.

Please come back.

Jaime inhaled a shaky breath and wished she could hug her own daughter. She understood Melinda's fear of discovery. She agonized until the moment she had to tell her parents she was pregnant with Ella. No one raised a voice or a hand. Her parents wouldn't do that. But they did display stoic disappointment. That hurt worse than any words or hands could.

"I wonder where Jeremiah was during this time," Jaime said as she leaned in closer to Drew.

"I don't know. The letter I read made it sound like Melinda was forbidden to see him." Drew curled an arm around her. "This sounds like this might be one of the later letters." He hunched forward. "Does it say anything about a curse?"

Jaime skimmed the rest of the letter. "No. She goes on to tell Jeremiah about her day and how her father chose a suitor for her." She glanced at the date. "May 19, 1917." With slow, deliberate moves, she folded the letter and set it aside. She selected another letter from the pile, cleared her throat, and read aloud.

My Dearest,

Two months have passed, and my heart still aches for your daddy. He was all of the best parts of me rolled into one. I still can't believe he's gone. He should be here. We should be celebrating our marriage. Instead, he left me alone.

I can't forgive my daddy. I know the Lord says you're supposed to, but I don't know if I can. I hope the Lord can forgive me for what I did. I can't bring myself to tell you. I don't want you to think the worst of me. Just know that what I did was out of love and protection for you.

Who will you be? Mama says it's too early to feel anything, but I swear I feel you inside of me. Will you be a boy with bright hazel eyes, like your daddy? Or will you be a girl with my red hair and blue eyes?

I'm fighting to keep you, but I don't know how I'm going to do it. Aunt Betsy says I've sinned, and I shouldn't keep you. She's heard about places down in the city where a girl like me can take care of her problem, and then come home before anybody in the town knows what she did. I won't go. You're a piece of Jeremiah. You and his fiddle. I can't give either one of you up.

I'm going to figure something out. I don't know what yet. Maybe I can slip away to Boone or Asheville. Maybe clear down to Raleigh. I hear they have jobs for girls. I don't know what I'll do yet, but I do know I'm keeping you. Let the town talk. I don't care. You're mine.

Love,

Your Mama

Jaime's breath hitched as she wiped at her damp eyes. "This one isn't even for Jeremiah. It was written for her son." She studied the date. "October 12, 1917. Five months after the last letter."

"So, that means Jeremiah died in sometime in between. Wait a minute." Drew rummaged in the bag and retrieved a piece of paper. He unfolded it, smoothing it flat. His family tree from the ancestry site filled the page. "Thomas was born on January 8, 1918." He lifted his head, his hazel eyes deep in thought. "Jeremiah never saw his son."

"That's awful."

Melinda's story resembled her own. A single woman, raising a child alone. Braden lived somewhere else in the world, but he had made it clear he didn't want to be a father at nineteen. She didn't blame him for taking off and transferring to another school now. However, she hated him for years when she found out. But after a while, she understood how scared and freaked out he felt. She imagined Jeremiah reacted in a different way and wanted to be a father. He would have stayed by Melinda's side if he had the choice.

Like Melinda, Jaime refused to give away her child. Ella became the most important thing in her life, and she never regretted a moment, even when her parents tossed her disappointed looks and worried what the neighbors might think.

For all of their modern thinking, they held old-fashioned values about single young mothers. But her mother came around when she saw a vision of Ella before she entered the world.

Did Melinda's family come around when they met her baby?

Jaime wanted to know more about the sin Melinda claimed she committed. It didn't sound like she referred to her pregnancy. And what town had they lived in?

"Are you okay?" Drew moved closer and wiped one of her tears away with his thumb.

"Yeah." Jaime laughed a little as she dabbed her own eyes. "Just relating to Melinda. It's one thing to dream about the woman, wondering if your own imagination created her. It's another to actually read her words."

"How hard was it? Taking care of Ella on your own?" His expression turned serious.

Jaime set down the letter and took a deep breath. "Hard, but I wasn't alone. My dad wasn't happy and spent most of the time not speaking to me. But my mom helped. They were both disappointed in me. Education is the number one thing in my family. But my mom sort of fell in love with Ella and seemed to forgive me a lot quicker." She tapped the letter. "I hope Melinda's mother forgave her."

"I do, too." Drew let out a breath. "I'm sorry my family brought all this danger to yours. That's not what I had in mind when we started dating." He straightened. "Not what I had in mind when I kissed you." He crept closer and took her hand. "I think we should make this official."

A slow smile spread across Jaime's lips. "Make what official?"

"This. This whole thing." Drew waved his hand around. "You and me. A couple." The sly grin returned, warming Drew's features. "I love you."

She sobered. "That's a big word, Drew. You can't throw it around like that. Besides, it won't be just the two of us." Her first instinct made her want to shut it down. She couldn't let another man break Ella's heart. Honestly, she couldn't let another man break hers. "I'm a packaged deal."

Drew arched a brow. "I want you in my life, Jaime. You and Ella."

Her heart cracked open and let a little hope inside. "It's a big responsibility. You're so much younger than I am. Most men…"

"I'm not most men, and there's only a four-year difference," he interrupted. "Please. Let's give this a shot. I want this to be serious. You, Ella, and me."

Jaime didn't know what to say. The rational side of her wanted to tell him no. That once they destroyed the curse, she and her daughter would go. But her heart stopped her from saying the words. And, oh, shouldn't she give into her heart at least once?

She pressed her lips to his, tentative at first. A light flutter against warmth. He cradled her head in his hands, and the kiss deepened. Then she drowned in him. The taste of peppermint lingered on her tongue, and she craved more of it. She wrapped her arms around his neck and pressed against him. Her heart quickened as the whole world seemed to stop.

His hands, callused from working with machine parts, roamed from her face down her neck to her breasts. He cupped them. Excitement zinged from the place where his hands touched. Her breath caught.

She moved away from his mouth, dropping kisses on his cheek, his prickly, stubbled chin. She trailed kisses down his neck. Her fingers pulled at his shirt, a cloth-made barrier between them.

"Do you?" he asked.

"Yes." Her brain formed that one word. Yes, yes, a thousand times, yes. Jaime didn't want to play it cautious and safe. She loved this man, and she ached to trust him with all of her. Why had it taken her so long?

Drew swept her into his arms and carried her upstairs to her room. For one night only, Jaime chose to give into her heart's demands. And her heart hungered for Drew. No curses, no shadow ghosts, nothing but the two of them.

19

Drew placed Jaime on the soft bed. With an impish grin, he reached one hand under her shirt and lightly traced her stomach with his fingers. Jaime trembled, goosebumps traveling all over her body. She pulled him down to her, taking his mouth. His lips, soft and steady, opened, his tongue twisting around hers.

"These clothes are in my way." Jaime yanked on his shirt.

Drew moved back. "Patience." His nimble fingers worked at the button on her jeans. He then meticulously unzipped them.

Jaime lifted her hips, her pulse picking up speed. Warmth flushed her whole body. She struggled to remember the last time she'd been with a caring and careful man.

Drew slid her jeans off and discarded them to the side. He chuckled as he slid her panties off. "Green. My favorite color." The panties went the way of the jeans. He lowered his head between her legs and planted light kisses on the inside of her thighs. He licked each spot with his tongue after each kiss.

Jaime bit her bottom lip. What a glorious, amazing feeling! But she bet he planned much, much more. Drew moved up, up, until glorious sensations filled every part of her. Jaime gasped. It really had been too long.

She moaned as he teased and played. Her hips moved with the rhythm he set. She let her head fall back and closed her eyes. Each kiss, each touch, brought her closer to the edge. Her body hungered for more.

"Do you like that?" Drew asked.

Jaime opened her eyes, peering down into his soft hazel ones. "Yes." The only word she could utter.

As soon as he brought her close enough, he slid away. She shivered in his absence. His clothes followed hers, and lastly, the rest of her clothes joined the pile.

"I hope you brought protection," Jaime said.

"Of course." Drew took her mouth in a deep, fiery kiss. He embraced her, nestling her closer to his heat.

She molded against him as if she had always belonged there. She kissed his shoulders, his neck, the stubble on his jaw, everywhere. His mouth trailed kisses down from her mouth to her breasts. Taking one in, he sucked and licked. Jaime's breath caught in her throat.

Finally, he entered her, and together, they moved to their own soft music. With each thrust, Jaime fought not to cry out. She held onto him and rode it until she thought her heart would burst from her chest. She climbed and climbed until she reached the peak. Every nerve ending stood on end as she climbed and leapt off the cliff.

As she caught her breath, Jaime rested her head on Drew's shoulder.

"You're not good for me," she said.

"Why?"

"Because I can't keep myself from falling in love with you."

Drew pushed a lock of hair behind her ear. "Good. Because I'm already in love with you."

Jaime was tucked in so warm and safe that it took her longer than usual to realize she was walking in Melinda's forest again. She stood at the edge of the clearing, which appeared smaller than it had during her previous visits. She stepped from the cool dark of the woods into the pleasant circle of light. In a few strides, she climbed onto the creaky porch. The door to the cabin opened, and Melinda emerged. She wore her long red hair down past her shoulders, and her eyes brightened when she saw Jaime.

"I can see the love pouring off you," she said, closing the door behind her.

"Am I that obvious?" Jaime peered down at her own nightshirt and pants, an outfit she didn't remember putting on. Maybe her dreamself tried to retain a little modesty.

"To me, anyway." Melinda lifted her skirts and walked out into the light. "I have something to show you. I wanted to wait until I knew you were the one and until I knew you'd understand." She headed around the side of the cabin.

Jaime hurried to catch up with her. "I read some of your letters. I'm sorry for your loss."

"Thank you. I appreciate that." Melinda cut another corner, making her way to the back of the cabin. "It's been a long time since I've seen him."

"I can't imagine a loss like that." Even the mere thought of losing Ella, or now even losing Drew, caused a sadness to creep in.

Melinda stopped at the edge of the clearing. "Don't dwell on that. You and my blood are going to make it right." She pointed to the dark woods in front of them. Another light appeared over a small group of trees and a river. Off to the right, a waterfall appeared. Rushing water filled Jaime's ears. "This is what you're fighting for."

Two young women raced into the other circle of light, breathing heavily. Their long blue skirts bunch in their hands, and their hats were slightly askew. They both shared bright red hair and ivory skin. They stopped next to a tree, laughing. One of them caught a branch in her hand as she tried to slow her breathing.

"You beat me again, Esther." The taller of the two said. She leaned against the tree and fanned her face. "I think you're cheating."

"I am not." Esther drew herself up to her full height as she released the branch. "I won fair and square like I always do. You're just too slow, Melinda."

"Melinda?" Jaime glanced at the woman standing next to her. Melinda nodded. Jaime saw the likeness between the older woman and the younger version of herself in the trees.

Younger Melinda inhaled a deep breath and pressed a hand to her chest. "I'm going to miss these races."

"What do you mean, 'miss'? You're not going anywhere." Esther bent down to the river and pushed up her sleeves. She dunked her hands into the water, cupped the liquid, and splashed her face.

"I'm almost eighteen. Daddy says I have to act like a young woman now and marry well. He introduced me to Mr. Clarence Smith the other day."

Esther wrinkled her small nose. "That boring gentleman he brought to dinner? The banker?"

"Yes. He wants to court me, and Daddy wants him to." Melinda studied her nails.

"Do you want to?"

"I don't know what I want."

At that moment, fiddle music filled the forest. The fiddler played the tune quick and fast. It bounced off the forest, dancing through the leaves. Younger Melinda pushed away from the tree.

"Do you hear that?" She exchanged a glance with her sister. Her face beamed as her toes tapped against the dirty ground.

Esther stood, and they followed the sound down the river, closer to the waterfall.

Younger Melinda gasped when she saw the player. Jaime did, too, because she recognized him as the ghost haunting her house. But in this scene, he stood solid and in full color. He was tall and lean, with blond hair falling over his forehead. He held the bow in light fingers as it jumped across the strings of his fiddle, the same fiddle that Jaime had hung in her living room. The same one that tried to tempt Drew to his death. The young man played for a few moments more before he stopped and raised his head. He noticed how the two young women watched him.

"Hello, there," he said, his words musical with his thick, Irish accent.

"Hello," Esther said, nudging her sister.

Younger Melinda couldn't seem to form words. She only stared at him.

"What are you playing?" Esther took a step closer to him.

"A jig my da taught me. I play it when I'm homesick, and it makes me feel better."

"It's lovely." Younger Melinda finally found her voice. "Where are you from?"

"Dublin, Ireland." He lowered the fiddle and the bow.

"That's so far away!" Esther exclaimed. "How did you wind up in Frost Gap?"

Jaime covered her mouth. Frost Gap. That was the name of the town. It was a clue. A tangible, real clue. She glanced at Melinda, who merely smiled.

"Why didn't you tell me?" Jaime asked.

Melinda lowered her head. "It's part of the curse. He won't allow me."

"But you were able to do this." Jaime smiled knowingly.

"Yes." Melinda offered no further explanation.

Jaime turned her attention back to the scene in front of her. Jeremiah ambled toward young Melinda and her sister, his fiddle swinging from his left hand and his bow dangling from his right. A smile broke out across his face, and Jaime's stomach flipped. He and Drew shared the same smile.

"My cousin lives here. I'm Jeremiah, by the way." He spoke to both girls, but he focused on young Melinda.

Melinda's cheeks reddened. She giggled as she introduced herself and her sister, working up the courage to talk to him.

The scene went dark for a moment.

Jaime turned to her companion. "You didn't meet him at a church picnic like the legend said?"

Melinda laughed. "Nor was I as brave as it paints me. People like to embellish the truth." She nodded to the patch of woods.

When the light came back, only Melinda and Jeremiah stood beside the waterfall. Their hands joined. He wore his overalls and work shirt, while Melinda looked lovely in a simple, long brown skirt and white shirtwaist. She wore her hair in a small bun.

She dipped her head, her expression strained.

"He'll know I'm gone and will come looking for me at any moment." Melinda glanced over her shoulder.

"I'm going to prove I'm a good match for you. He won't stand in the way." Jeremiah held her chin between his thumb and fingers and turned her head to face him. "I won't quit without a fight."

"You don't know him. My daddy always gets his way." Fear laced Melinda's words.

"I'm not afraid of your da. It's going to be all right. I promise."

Melinda yanked her hand out of his and stepped back. She covered her stomach. "You can't promise that. When he finds out about this, about us, he'll kill you and me." She looked down. "And our baby."

"Nothing will happen to you. You have my word, mo grá." He reached for her, but she moved away.

"Let's run away tonight. To somewhere he won't find us." Melinda twisted her skirt around her fingers.

Jeremiah shook his head. "No. I'm going to do this right. I'm going to make this right."

The light winked out, leaving a dark forest. The ground rumbled beneath Jaime and Melinda as the air grew colder. Melinda pushed Jaime away.

"Go. He's coming. Go!"

Jaime shot straight up. She blinked as her eyes adjusted to the morning light shining through the window. Drew still slept next to her. He lay peacefully on his stomach, safe and unharmed, snoring.

Jaime took a deep breath and then another as she calmed her racing heart. A waterfall in Frost Gap. That's where they needed to break the curse. She tossed the covers aside and headed for her computer, determined to narrow it down.

***

Drew's eyes fluttered open. For a moment, he had no idea where he was. Strange bed, strange room. No one slept beside him. Memories of the previous night flooded back of Jaime, naked and in his arms.

He gathered his clothes and dressed. Heading downstairs, he found Jaime on the couch with her laptop open.

"Morning!" he called.

"Hi!" Jaime kept her eyes on the screen.

"Find anything good?"

She sighed as she turned off her laptop, clicking it closed. "I think I may have found something, but I don't think it's enough. There's coffee in the kitchen if you want it."

Drew grabbed a cup before joining her on the couch. After the night they enjoyed, he expected her to be more relaxed. Maybe even in the mood to do it all again. But

Jaime's shoulders tensed as she chewed on the end of her thumb.

"What's wrong?" he asked as he set his mug down.

"I dreamed about Melinda again." She told him about seeing how Melinda and Jeremiah met, and more importantly, where they kept meeting. A waterfall near a town called Frost Gap.

"I've never heard of the place, and I've lived in the Blue Ridge Mountains my whole life." Drew sipped the hot, rich coffee. He curled his fingers around the mug, heating them.

"It's not on a map, either. But I did come across a legend that's from your neck of the woods."

Drew raised his brows. "Yeah?"

"Yeah. Apparently, in a forest on the outskirts of Boone, a female ghost wanders the trees at night. The legend is she's searching for her lover."

Drew nodded. "They all are. It's a pretty generic legend."

Jaime tucked her legs under her. "But it might be the right place to look. I couldn't see anything on the map, but maybe I can find something in the archives at the college. Blackwood has a lot of old newspapers. Maybe something mentions Frost Gap or a waterfall near there."

"You know what I think?" Drew set down his half-finished mug and shifted closer to Jaime. He kissed her neck. "I think we need to stop thinking and worrying for a while." He nibbled the soft lobe of her ear. "When does Ella get home?"

Jaime giggled. "Not until three this afternoon."

"Perfect. Because I have an excellent idea about how we can spend the time." He kissed her mouth, his lips parting. She answered, letting her tongue dart and play.

When they came up for air, all she said was, "Perfect."

20

Drew sauntered down the hall to his apartment, his key in his hand and the bag with the box of letters in the other. He hummed a little tune as he went along. For the first time in a long time, he felt happy. Really, really happy. He wanted to skip, sing, and shout from the rooftops. He and Jaime had found a place where Melinda and Jeremiah could have met, even if they weren't quite sure where to locate it. And even better than that, he and Jaime belonged each other. Drew didn't remember feeling this way about any woman. Jaime gave him the confidence to not only take on the curse, but the world as well.

Ella reacted in a negative way, though. She didn't seem all that glad to find Drew with Jaime when she got home from her sleepover. She mumbled a quick hello before darting to her room and shutting the door. Drew sighed. He hoped he could win her over, too.

What are you doing? A tiny voice in the back of his mind asked. *You've got a curse to break. You don't have time to make commitments. What if the shadow wins? How will you keep your commitment then? And even worse, what if the shadow hurts or kills Jaime and Ella, too?* Drew slowed as he let the doubts seep in. The voice told the truth. What was he thinking? Despite Jaime's dreams and Ella's psychic connection to the bow, he wanted to keep them as far away from this as possible. He made a promise to them, but maybe he hadn't chosen the wisest move?

Plus, like Jaime said, she came as a packaged deal. Was he even ready to be a father? He didn't know the first thing about how to do that, especially since he couldn't point to a great role model. Did Ella even want him around? Based on her actions, the answer was a clear and resounding no.

Drew stopped humming as his mood took a dive. Reality setting in made everything worse.

"There you are!" Tabitha stood at his door, a black cloth bag hanging from her shoulder. "I've been texting and calling you all afternoon."

"You did?" Drew pulled out his phone. A string of missed texts and calls from Tabitha bounced through the screen. "Oh, man, I'm sorry. I set it to vibrate. I was with Jaime."

"Oh?" Tabitha seemed to relax as a smile crossed her face. "Oh! Well, in that case, you're forgiven."

"Is everything okay? Did I miss anything important?" Dread pooled in his stomach. "The shadow didn't get out, did it?"

"No, no, everyone's fine. Lisa came by this morning and brought your part." Tabitha patted the bag.

"Awesome!" Drew unlocked his door. "Come on in and let's have a look." He led the way into the apartment and set the box of letters on his small table in the corner. "Tell her thank you for me. I hope it wasn't too much trouble."

"It took some convincing, and a promise of a favor, but I wouldn't call it trouble." Tabitha handed the bag to Drew. "What is that?" She pointed to the box of letters.

"A present from my family." He explained the love letters inside, which led to Jaime's dream and Frost Gap.

Tabitha stuffed her hands into her coat pocket. "I feel like we haven't done enough to help you with this."

Drew held up the bag. "This is amazing." He carefully removed a short, narrow box. Resting it on the table, he opened it to reveal a tube right out of science fiction.

"Is that the Klystron thingy?" Tabitha asked.

"It is."

"I thought it would be bigger."

"Some of them are. But this one is the perfect size to try and stop ghosts." He cradled it, studying every feature. "I think it's going to work better than the EMP generator. At least it shouldn't knock out all the power. It should generate power at a lower setting."

"That'll be a relief. I know it'll make Aaron happy."

Drew placed the emitter back into its box. "What favor did you promise Lisa?"

"It's not a big deal." Tabitha tried to wave it off and change the subject. "Tell me how we're going to break your curse."

Drew arched an eyebrow. He had never spent much time with Tabitha one-on-one before. Aaron and McKenna hung around with them most of the time. But he had a feeling they came from similar backgrounds. Drew had his mother and sister to rely on, and he didn't think Tabitha could say the same. He often wondered if Aaron, McKenna, and he created the family she relied on. She held secrets and personal tidbits close to her chest.

She sighed as she shrugged out of her coat. "It was more of a general favor. A promise that if she asked me to help with something at the Institute, I would." She draped her coat on the back of the nearest chair, careful not to meet Drew's eyes.

"You promised to do something for the Institute you walked away from? You did that for me?" He felt touched, but also a little angry. Yes, he wanted to make a better version of the ghost disruptor—one that would be easier to use than tossing salt all over the place and might keep the shadow at bay long enough to break the curse. But he didn't want one of his closest friends to make a deal with the devil to do it.

"Of course. You're like my little brother. The first time I saw that shadow try to kill you, it scared me to death. I don't want to lose you. So, yes, if this part helps you create something that'll stop that monster, then I'll owe my sister a favor." Tabitha pressed her lips together and stuck out her chin. She was tiny, but fierce.

"Thank you. That means a lot." He tugged her into a hug. "But whatever this favor turns out to be, I'm going to help you pay it back." He stepped away. "You've got a little brother who will back you up. You won't do it alone."

Tabitha laughed. "Are you kidding? Aaron blew his top when he found out what I did. Trust me, he won't let me do it alone." She dusted her hands. "So, where do we start?"

"You want to help?"

"If I can."

"Okay." Drew dug out the drawing of his prototype, and the two of them went to work.

Jaime squirmed in the uncomfortable microfilm machine chair as she flipped through old newspapers. The dusty smell of the old magazines and newspapers filled the wall behind her while the cold, metal boxes that held the microfilms covered the rest of the space. A couple of students studied at the carrels nearby, the occasional shuffle of a flipped page disrupting the silence. Otherwise, quiet descended on the basement of the Blackwood College library. Nothing but the swishing whir of the machine as she turned the black dial to click through the images.

She loved searching through old articles and primary sources, but her eyes ached from staring at the images on the screen for a long time.

Unfortunately, Frost Gap was no longer a town. From what Jaime could tell, the town boasted a tiny Main Street with a post office and a general store and not much else. Over time, people moved away to search for jobs in larger towns and cities, and Boone, Blowing Rock, and other nearby places incorporated parts of it. She found a few old, broken cabins and some ruins on an internet map, but that was all that remained. She had a general idea of where to go, but a lot of forests covered the area. And several waterfalls stood in many of those forests and wooded areas. Any one of them could have been where Melinda and Jeremiah met and fell in love.

All of this led her to the microfilm machine and old local newspapers, hoping for anything that might shed some light on Melinda's so-called sin. She sounded afraid in the letter, and even more so in the dreams. Jaime accepted that whatever Melinda had done helped curse the fiddle. She hoped they might use the information to break it. So far, she identified no handy knowledge.

She sighed, sat back, and rubbed her burning eyes. She focused on the wall behind the machine. Maybe the letters would offer Drew a better clue.

"You ready for a Mountain Dew break?" Tristan leaned on her machine, his green eyes bright.

"Hey." Jaime blinked. "Don't you have a class to teach?"

"Taught it and killed it."

"Huh? What time is it?" She fished out her phone. Ten

forty-five beamed on her screen. "Crap. I missed my morning classes." She liked to schedule the classes she took as a student in the mornings when she could.

Tristan tapped the top of the machine. "You've been in your own little world lately. I haven't talked to you or Drew. What's going on?"

Jaime filled him in on the letters and her search. "I think if I can find out what Melinda did, I can figure out how we break the curse."

"Okay." Tristan knelt down beside her. "You have a name and a place. What do you need now?"

"I don't know." She stretched her tired arms and aching back, which made a satisfying pop. She realized she had sat in that seat for a long time. "I was hoping there might be a mention of her or her father, Richard Beauchamp." She bit her bottom lip. "If I brought you the letters…"

"It doesn't work that way." Tristan turned the black knob, clicking through pages one at a time. "I pick up things from places and people, not objects."

"But you picked up the history of the fiddle." Jaime wrinkled her brow, exhaustion kicking in.

"No, I picked up the ghost. Jeremiah. His energy was strong."

"Oh." Her hope deflated, but then she remembered his vision. "Wait. You said you saw Jeremiah get shot. That must be how he died. Did you see who did it?"

Tristan furrowed his brow. "All I saw was the barrel of the shot gun pointed at me seconds before it went off. I didn't see a face."

"Well, Jeremiah is still hanging out at my house if you want to try again."

Tristan seemed to consider it. "I could try again, but how will that help break the curse?"

"I'm not sure." Jaime tapped her fingers on the microfilm

machine. "I'm hoping that if we know how Jeremiah died it might shed some light on how his death created a curse. Neither my dreams nor Drew's letters have shed any light in that area." She slid down in the chair, realizing none of the research seemed to help. She groaned.

"At least you don't have a deadline," Tristan offered.

"That just makes it worse. How long can that fiddle stay locked away in the Restless Spirits' office? And more importantly, how long will my daughter keep having visions about a box holding a bow?" She crossed her arms. "I want this done and over with. If you can't magically find my answers, I guess we have to find the answers the old-fashioned way." She blew out a breath. "Thorough research."

"You like research." He nudged her shoulder.

Jaime grinned. "I do, but the ghost is still in my house, and the shadow keeps stalking Drew."

Tristan drew his lips together in a straight line. "Drew didn't mention that to me." He dipped his dark eyebrows down.

"Some psychic you are."

"Funny. I read the past, not minds."

The joke brought a little lightness to Jaime's mood. She chuckled as she glanced back at the screen. A name caught her eye. "Stop!"

Tristan did so.

Jaime zoomed in on a story in the corner. BELOVED FROST GAP MAYOR DIES UNEXPECTEDLY. "According to the article, Mayor Richard Beauchamp died in a hunting accident on August 8, 1917." She leaned in closer and skimmed the rest of the article. "No one knew who pulled the trigger, but he appeared to die from a shotgun wound to the chest. His wife said that she didn't realize he had gone hunting that day. He was survived by his wife and his two daughters, Melinda and Esther."

"It's an obituary," Tristan said. "What's so special about it?"

Jaime wasn't listening. She flipped through her handwritten notes, Mayor Beauchamp's death date ringing in her head. Finally, she found the reason why it sounded familiar. Jeremiah Keane died the same month and year, also from a shotgun wound. "This is." She showed the date to Tristan.

"You have a month and year that matches, but no definite date," Tristan pointed out.

"I know, but it has to mean something." She skimmed the other articles, but they didn't mention Jeremiah anywhere.

"Wait a minute. He looks familiar." Tristan pointed to the picture next to the article. "That's Richard Beauchamp, right? I think I saw him in my vision." His green eyes widened. "I think he held the shotgun."

"Are you sure? You said all you saw was the barrel." Jaime tapped the end of her pen on her notebook. The pace went faster the more excited she got.

"I know. I did think that's all I saw, until I saw the picture. It's grainy, but I remember him."

"So, he shot Jeremiah, which means Jeremiah didn't shoot him." Jaime stopped tapping the end of her pen and started chewing it instead. "Then who shot Richard?"

Tristan closed his eyes and his brow furrowed. "I remember seeing him and the girl with the long, red hair. I was seeing everything from Jeremiah's point of view. Those were the only people I saw." He opened his eyes. "I'm sorry I'm not more help."

"Wait." The wheels in Jaime's head turned as pieces fit together. The legend Laurie shared with her and Drew returned to her in bits. The young woman grabbed the shotgun and shot her father. She wanted to dismiss it, recalling Melinda's words about people embellishing the truth, but she refused to deny it.

According to Tristan's vision, Melinda, Jeremiah, and her father met in the woods alone. Melinda claimed a sin that caused her shame, one she couldn't seem to confess to her son. Richard killed Jeremiah, and he died from a gun shot in the same month and year. Possibly the same day. Jaime's hand flew to her mouth. "I think Melinda killed her father with his own gun. Her guilt, his anger. That might be enough to make a curse, right?"

Tristan rubbed his stubbly chin. "I don't know. I'm clueless when it comes to curses, but you might be onto something."

"I bet your girlfriend would know." Jaime hovered the box around the article and hit the print button.

"That is a possibility, but you have a class to teach this afternoon."

Jaime grimaced. He was right. She didn't have time for classes. She needed to save her daughter and Drew.

Tristan waved his cell phone. "Let's see what she has to say."

They made their way out of the basement of the library and into the bright, cold autumn sun. Jaime pulled her coat tighter around her, breathing in the crisp air. Her earlier sleepiness gave way to a renewed energy. She wanted Jeremiah's ghost gone from her house and Ella's life before the Thanksgiving holiday, which remained a couple of weeks away. With her new theory, she believed they could do it.

"Tristan! Your timing is awesome. I was getting ready to call you." McKenna's tinny voice drifted from Tristan's phone's speakers.

"What's wrong?" Tristan stopped walking.

"How can you tell something's wrong?"

"Your voice has that slight high-pitched sound to it."

Jaime edged closer to the phone. "What's going on?"

"Jaime! You're there, too. Good."

"Don't tell her." Drew's rumble interrupted McKenna.

"Tell me what?" Her stomach twisted into a knot.

"It's nothing," he answered. "How's the research going?"

"Like hell it's nothing." Jaime gripped the phone and Tristan's hand. Students and faculty walking by glanced at them. "Something happened. What?"

"Tell her," McKenna admonished. "Or I will."

"Traitor." Drew grumbled. "The shadow attacked me again."

"Are you in your office?" Fear clawed at her.

"Yes. I was trying something."

"He was being stupid," McKenna chimed in.

"I'm coming down there. I'll talk to Dr. Cameron and get the rest of the day off." Jaime released Tristan's hand and his phone. She turned on her heel, ready to march back to the history building.

"I'm coming, too." She heard three heavy steps before Tristan matched her pace. With his long legs, it wasn't hard to do.

Fallen leaves crunched under their feet as they headed across the quad.

"You don't have to do that. I'm fine. We're all fine." Jaime pictured Drew waving his hands in the air and trying to act like none of this bothered him.

"I think it's good you're coming," McKenna said.

"I don't need your help, Mac," Drew grumbled.

"You're holding my phone, Drew," McKenna snapped.

Jaime and her quickened pace neared the history building when her own phone rang in her pocket. She retrieved it and recognized the school's number. Her pulse jumped. "Give me a minute." She moved away from Tristan to answer it.

"Ms. Liu, this is Mrs. Wells, Ella's teacher. I'm glad I could reach you." The woman on the other end sounded breathless.

"Yes, I remember. Is everything okay?" Her heart quickened its rhythm.

"It's Ella. She passed out in class today and started mumbling about a box in the woods. She's with the nurse now."

Jaime tipped against the closest brick wall, her hand breaking the fall. She hoped her knees wouldn't give out. "Is she okay?"

"It's probably best if you come pick her up."

Jaime swallowed her fears. "I'm on my way."

21

Drew and Tabitha worked past dinnertime. He led the project, explaining what piece needed to go where. She listened and followed his directions to the letter. A comfortable silence settled between them as they built the new version of the ghost disruptor. Drew praised Tabitha's assistance, and she waved him off, claiming modesty. She left sometime around eight.

Drew continued to perfect and tweak the ghost disruptor 2.0 until he couldn't hold his eyes open anymore. But he set his alarm early for the next day because he had formed a plan.

It probably wouldn't hold the number one spot of great plans, but he grinned when he thought about it, focusing on the positive aspects.

Early the next morning, Drew took the new and improved disruptor to the office before anyone was due to be there. The fiddle called to him the moment he walked through the door. How had the urge to be near it grown so much in the time he'd been away from it? He almost lost his resolve as the door swung shut behind him, slamming loud enough to echo off the walls. He swallowed, concentrating on the weight of the disruptor in his hand.

Like the previous model, it was shaped like a science fiction ray gun, but this one boasted a sleeker look. The handle curved down a little longer to hold the battery pack on the end. He encased all the important inner parts in a green and black packaging, a new design Tabitha suggested.

When he turned it on the night before, it didn't take as long to charge. It also didn't mess with any other electrical equipment. He had tossed his hands into the air. "It's alive! It's alive!"

He had only completed one part of the test, however. He had to test it on a ghost to make sure it worked. A saner person would have gone to Jaime's house and tried it out on Jeremiah's ghost. But Drew never claimed to be a saner person. He didn't create the disruptor for ghosts like Jeremiah, trapped souls that meant no harm. No, he built it for entities like the shadow. Entities that held so much hate and anger, they wanted to kill. The little gun in his hand offered quicker protection than a bag of salt.

Drew walked forward on unsteady legs. The want, the need for the instrument wormed into his mind. He fought it and tried to ignore it as he crept into Aaron's office. He had a job to do, and he planned to do it, no matter what.

He opened the closet door. The fiddle's power packed a punch so big he wobbled on his feet. He blew out a breath as he gripped the doorknob, his knees weakening. Ominous laughter filled the space.

"I knew you'd be back." The voice filled the room.

Drew saw the tendrils of black fog writhing around the fiddle, pushing against its salt prison. He thanked everything and everyone he knew the white, grainy circle still held it in place.

His hands itched to hold the instrument, cradle it against

him. He ached to feel the smooth wood, the taut wire strings. He wanted to hold it, to play it, and to hear music pour from it. He gripped the disruptor, the smooth metal and plastic in his hand grounding him. Technology was his gift, not music. He had to remind himself.

"Come on, boy. Give in."

If he was going to test his new weapon, Drew knew he had to let the shadow out. Steeling himself, he pushed his foot through the circle, breaking the salt line.

He uncurled his fingers from the knob one at a time. Clutching the disruptor in one hand, he reached with the other and picked up the fiddle. His fingers tightened on the neck of the instrument, finding comfort there.

"That's it, boy. Give in."

Then the cold rushed in, pitch black darkness following in its wake. It squeezed and pressed. The peace vanished, and Drew struggled in a storm of darkness. A deep laugh echoed all around him. The frigid blackness gripped his throat. It squeezed and crushed. It cut off the air, none of it reaching Drew's lungs. He dropped the fiddle while he gasped and clawed at his throat. Stars dotted his vision.

He lifted the disruptor, fighting the resistance in his arm, and pointed it. His finger itched to flip the switch. But a strand of darkness knocked it out of his hand. It skittered across the floor, landing at the far end of the office.

Oh, shit, Drew thought. His heart thudded in his chest as he landed hard on his knees. Despair and fear shoved through. The shadow won. He tried to scream, but nothing came out. The dark closed around him, blocking out all the light. It was too late.

All of a sudden, light pierced the dark. Dots of light, to be precise. The shadow howled and released its hold on Drew's throat. It broke apart in an instant. The tiny bits of smoke left retreated into the fiddle.

A set of arms hooked around his shoulders and dragged him backward out of the closet. He stumbled through a door, blinking in the early morning sunlight. His back rested on a scratchy surface while three faces peered down at him.

"Drew? Are you okay?" McKenna's warm hand was at the side of his throat. "Drew?"

Drew breathed in and coughed. He wasn't dying. He lay on Aaron's office floor with his co-workers exchanging worried glances. Burning fire filled his throat. "How did you stop it?" he rasped. He grabbed Aaron's offered hand and allowed the other man to pull him into a sitting position.

Tabitha held up the disruptor and blew on the end of it. "Someone made an excellent weapon."

"It worked?" Another racking cough. "It really worked?"

"You should've told us you were planning on testing it." She lifted a perfectly shaped eyebrow.

Drew pressed his back against the hard desk, trying to catch his breath. Cool, crisp air flew past his lips. His knees ached. "How did you know I was here?"

"McKenna called us and said the front door was open." Aaron sat next to him, his back against the wall. "We were already on our way."

McKenna continued the story. "I felt anger and ice cold coming from this office. I thought someone was robbing the place. Then I felt you, but your emotions were so faint. I tried to open the door, but it wouldn't budge."

Drew glanced at the office door to see someone had burst it open.

Aaron sighed. "Looks like I'm buying a new door."

"I didn't want anyone else to get hurt. I thought I could handle it." Drew climbed to his feet, and dizziness hit him in seconds. Tabitha and McKenna each caught an elbow and steered him to a nearby chair.

"That's the stupidest thing I've ever heard," Tabitha said as she helped lower him into the chair.

Aaron climbed to his feet. "We're a team, damn it. We don't go off solo." Aaron glared at the fiddle with a grim expression on his rugged face. It lay on the floor of the closet doorway, appearing innocent. "We can't keep that thing and wait for you to find a way to end that curse. We've got to get rid of it."

Unexplainable panic seized Drew. He grasped Aaron's coat. "You can't."

"It's still trying to kill you, and it might eventually succeed." Aaron pried Drew's hands off his jacket. "We're going to try salting and burning it today."

Drew leapt off the chair. He tackled Aaron to the ground, and they landed with a thud. "Like hell you are." He landed a solid punch in Aaron's stomach.

"Son of a bitch!" Aaron hissed. He yanked his fist back and punched Drew in the face.

Drew's head whipped back as blood spurted from his nose. Rolling off Aaron and onto the floor, he clutched his sore, aching nose. His earlier panic melted away as the pain registered.

Aaron held his stomach as he lay on his back. "What the hell?"

McKenna help Drew sit up again. She thrust a paper towel into his hand. He held it to his nose, trying to get the bleeding to stop. "I don't know," he said around the paper towel. "I can't let you try to destroy it again."

"Mac," Aaron growled.

"He's telling the truth. I've never felt that much panic come from him before." McKenna rubbed Drew's back.

Tabitha crouched next to her husband. "Let's all calm down. Drew, you've got to find a way to break that curse before it kills you."

"I know. I'm close." He pulled the paper towel away and touched his nose. He gasped at the tenderness, but the bleeding had stopped. "I know I have to find the bow and put the two pieces together. And it's somewhere in a place called Frost Gap, but I still don't know exactly where the bow is."

"Do you have any leads?" McKenna asked.

"My great-great grandparents' letters. Melinda met my great-great-grandfather near a waterfall somewhere near Frost Gap, but she didn't name it. It could be any number of waterfalls." He pulled a bruised knee to his chest and rested an arm on it. "Aaron, I'm sorry for attacking you."

Aaron waved at him. "I'll live." He groused. "We need to put salt around that damn thing before the shadow recovers." Aaron grunted as he stood. He popped his back and glared at Drew. "So, we can't threaten to destroy this thing. Somehow, it has its claws in you, and you go berserk." He dusted off his jeans. "We're hunting for that waterfall."

Drew also climbed to his feet, slower than Aaron. He placed his hand on the desk for balance, wincing at the pain radiating from every muscle. "I don't even know if that bow is at the waterfall. It could be a random clue." He raked a hand through his hair. "I'm hoping I can find a letter that focuses on the curse and tells me exactly where the bow is."

McKenna dusted off her own jeans. "In the meantime, has Ella had any more visions?"

Drew rubbed the back of his neck with his free hand, guilt gnawing at him. "I don't feel right pulling an innocent ten-year-old girl into this."

"I think she's already into it. The ghost came to her first, not you. That has to mean something." McKenna shook out her long hair as she looked up at Drew. "She's working really hard."

"No waterfall name yet?" Aaron asked.

"No." McKenna shook her head. "But we're working on it."

"Then, I guess all we have to go on is Frost Gap." Aaron walked around his desk and settled into his chair. "What's on the schedule today, gang?"

McKenna walked to her desk, and Drew hobbled behind her. She sat down and turned on her computer. Once it hummed, she brought up the schedule. "It's a light day today. I have potential client meetings at eleven and two. Mr. and Mrs. Fall are coming in at four to discuss the findings at their house from last week's investigation." She lifted her head. "We still have the footage to review from the small bed and breakfast. That's it."

"Oh, man." Drew tossed his head back and groaned. "I forgot about the bed and breakfast footage." He shook his head. "I'm forgetting a lot of stuff. Being away from work sucks."

"Well, you are cursed." Aaron leaned sideways and gave him a pointed look through the broken door.

Drew narrowed his eyes. "Not funny, man."

McKenna crossed her arms. "I wonder what Tristan's schedule is today. He does love research, and I'll bet you haven't told him any of this, have you?"

"You know how he feels about ghosts." Drew thought everyone needed to stop ganging up on him.

"Yeah, but I also know how he feels about his friends." She cradled her phone in her hand, her thumbs flying over the screen. "Besides, he prefers research to visions."

Drew groaned. "I'm going to watch the footage and worry about somebody else's ghost for a while." He got halfway to his office before he heard Jaime's voice come through McKenna's speaker phone. He closed his eyes when he realized McKenna had told her something happened to Drew.

He shuffled back over to her and tried to make Jaime believe it was no big deal. By the end of the call, Drew felt ridiculous.

Drew sank into a chair and rested his forehead on the smooth surface of McKenna's desk. "You didn't have to tell her. It's not like I'm five."

McKenna sighed. "Trust me. She'd want to know. She's an important part of your life, right?"

Drew raised his aching head. "She is, which is why I want her safely away from this."

"You love her!" McKenna dropped back in her chair. "I'll take that to mean she's at the top of your important people list."

"Can I please have my emotions to myself?" Drew lowered his head again.

"Buck up, Drew. It's going to be okay." Tabitha patted his back, confidence in her voice.

"I hope so." He directed his comment to the floor.

Ella slumped in the backseat. She had remained there since Jaime picked her up, but at least she was awake and alert. Jaime imagined all kinds of terrible scenarios before she walked into the nurse's office. She thought of Ella bleeding from a head wound or in a coma and unresponsive. The ideas grew worse and worse, and Jaime's stomach twisted into more knots. But Ella seemed fine and in one piece. Jaime had found Ella sitting in a chair with not a scratch on her.

According to the nurse, Ella hadn't fainted as much as slumped over her desk. Jaime spent the next few minutes answering questions about Ella getting enough sleep and enough to eat. Finally, she collected her daughter and left the school.

Jaime settled in the driver's seat, but the car engine stayed silent. They sat in the parking lot, neither one saying anything. Jaime wanted to give Ella the chance to open up to her, but the wait killed her. She gripped the steering wheel, letting her nerves calm.

She breathed in, ready to make the first move.

"I'm sorry." Ella's voice filled the empty space.

Jaime released the air she held in. "Sorry for what?"

"For making you come to get me."

Jaime turned in her seat so she could see her daughter. "You made yourself pass out so I'd come get you?"

"No." Ella shook her head.

"Then what happened? You can tell me anything, you know?" She patted Ella's knee.

"Okay, so Mrs. Wells was going over last night's math homework. So I thought I could practice." Ella sighed and dragged her eyes from the window.

"Practice?" Jaime dreaded where her daughter might be going with this conversation.

"Finding things, like McKenna taught me." She scooted to the edge of her seat, a brightness in her light brown eyes. "I told Kelly my secret, and we practiced all weekend. And I think I'm getting better at it. I found a necklace that she hid outside the house."

"So, you thought you'd practice locating the box? In the middle of class?"

"Yeah." Ella nodded. "I think that wooden box really wants me to find it."

"What do you mean?"

Ella fussed with a string at the end of her shirt. "I saw it for a split second before I passed out." She pulled, and the string unraveled a little.

Worry gnawed in Jaime's stomach. She stepped out of the driver's side and slid into the back with Ella. She rested her hand on top of her daughter's. "I don't think this is something you should play with. Not unsupervised." She fought not to voice her real fear, but the fact that Ella had a vision without being close to the ghost or the fiddle scared her.

"Are you mad?" Ella asked.

"No, baby. I'm scared. I don't know what any of this

means. But I'm not mad." Jaime kissed the top of Ella's head. "No one has written a book about what to do if your child is psychic. We're both learning as we go."

"It means we've got to help Jeremiah." Ella straightened, pushing her shoulders back. "I saw more of the woods this time. I think it's under a rock surrounded by four trees near a waterfall." Ella's brow wrinkled. "But that isn't much, is it?"

"It's enough." Jaime patted her daughter's shoulder, her stomach queasy from the concern.

All Jaime wanted was a normal life. She knew, with her mother's predictions, that Ella could develop a power, but she never thought about how to help her learn to control this possible power. Ten years later, she was facing it head on. She refused to turn away and leave her daughter alone with this.

"El, you're not the only one seeing things related to the fiddle." Jaime took a deep breath. "I keep dreaming about Jeremiah's wife. Her name was Melinda." Sitting in the cold backseat in the middle of an elementary school parking lot, Jaime told her daughter about Drew's letters and that she continued to have dreams about Melinda. Ella's eyes grew bigger and rounder with each sentence until Jaime thought they might pop out of her head. When she finished, she waited for her daughter's reaction.

"That's so cool!" Ella bounced in her seat. "That means we can all help Jeremiah and get rid of that shadow thing."

"We still don't know which waterfall it is or which four trees you saw." Jaime put a hand on each of her daughter's shoulders to calm her down. "I don't like the idea of you helping us break the curse. You could get hurt."

"But I can find the box with the bow in it. I can do it."

"We'll talk about this later." A message from McKenna pinged on her phone.

McKENNA: Everything is fine. Drew is doing better. We sent him home and resealed the fiddle. How is Ella? Tristan told me.

Jaime loved that McKenna thought to ask about her daughter.

JAIME: She's okay. Trying to practice on her own. But she saw the box without being near the fiddle or the ghost. I'm worried about this leap in her abilities.

McKENNA: I might have some answers. Tristan and I found something in his grandfather's journals that might explain the leap. I'd love to go over it with you.

JAIME: Are you free now?

McKENNA: Absolutely.

JAIME: We'll be there in a few minutes.

Jaime put away her phone and smiled at Ella. "McKenna said she might know what is making your powers grow."

"Okay."

With a nod, Jaime slid out of the back seat. She moved to the front, feeling better than she had earlier. She required something to focus on instead of all the uncertainty. She chose to deal with Ella now and talk to Drew later.

Minutes later, they perched in the big, leather chairs in the conference room at Restless Spirits with McKenna. Tristan was staying at the college to teach an upcoming class but joined them on McKenna's laptop.

After hearing Ella's story, McKenna sat back and ran her hands through her wavy brown hair. "Psychic powers can grow as we get older. When I was your age, I had to stand close to someone to tell what they were feeling. Now, I can do it across a crowded room. But my powers didn't grow this fast." She faced the laptop monitor. "Tristan?"

"Mine hit me like a one-two punch when they showed up. Not just seeing, but dropping me into the past." He held up an old book. "But I thought grandpa's journals might mention this."

"McKenna mentioned his journals to me. Why didn't you say something this morning?" Jaime rested her elbows on the table.

"You didn't ask." Tristan grinned.

Jaime narrowed her eyes. "You could have brought it up."

"In the middle of the library?"

Jaime continued to glare for a moment. "Good point."

"Besides, I didn't think about it until you got the call from Ella's school. That reminded me." Tristan opened the old leather-bound book. The pages crinkled as he flipped.

Jaime's inner-history geek itched to grab the journal and read it from cover to cover. "I'm surprised your grandfather wrote about stuff like this." Jaime exchanged a glance with McKenna.

"He worked for the Greene Institute back in the sixties, along with my grandmother. He kept journals about their experiences and their powers. Tristan's dad gave them to us when we were trying to stop The White Lady back in September," McKenna explained.

Ella beamed. "Your grandmother is psychic, too? So's mine."

McKenna raised quizzical dark brows.

"My mother can see a few hours into the future, and only in the area she's in," Jaime answered.

"And you?" McKenna asked.

"Other than the weird dreams about Drew's great-great grandmother, nothing." She shrugged. "I think it skips a generation in my family."

"That's interesting that Ella and your mother have different abilities. I don't think I've come across that before."

Tristan flipped through the pages of the book, crinkling sounds coming through the laptop. When he reached the page he seemed to be hunting for, he crowed. "Here it is! I knew I had seen something." He began to read. "'Diana had a strange experience today. Her ability to read minds seemed to grow overnight. We had spent the night in the house, waiting for the ghost to appear. Diana said she had seen the ghost that night. It had stayed by her bedside.'"

"Jeremiah does that sometimes." Ella sat straighter. "I'll wake up in the middle of the night, and he'll be there."

"He will?" Jaime regarded her daughter, surprised Ella hadn't told her this before.

"Yeah, but not in a creepy way. It's like he's keeping an eye out for the shadow, in case it comes back."

Tristan continued, "'Before the encounter with the ghost, she only read minds of people in the same room with her. Afterwards, I was outside the house, and she still heard what I was thinking. It gave her a headache. We sent her home, and within a day, her powers went back to normal levels. We think it was the proximity to the spirit that influenced her, but we don't know why it hasn't influenced the rest of us in the same way.

"'Lauren thinks it might have to do with Diana's age. She's the youngest of us at nineteen, and she hasn't settled fully into her powers yet.'"

"That sounds like Grandma," McKenna said.

"So, if your grandfather was right, Ella is having a sort of power spike whenever she's close to the ghost or the fiddle?" Jaime tapped her nails on the table.

"That's what it sounds like." Tristan closed the book. "And I think the only way to make it stop is to help Drew break the curse."

McKenna nodded. "I agree. You and Ella seem to be as much a part of this curse as he is."

Jaime shoved a hand through her hair. "That's all fine and good, but how does that explain what happened today?"

Tristan bowed to his girlfriend. "Mac, I'll let you take this one."

McKenna tilted back in her chair and bounced a little. "I honestly don't know. It could be all the practice. A muscle gets stronger when you work it. I think psychic powers might work the same way. And if Jeremiah's energy is still in your house, Ella has been exposed to it more than the girl Tristan's grandpa talked about."

Ella chewed her bottom lip, a dark expression on her face. She looked from Jaime to McKenna to Tristan on the monitor before her whole face lit up. "Cool."

"Not cool." Jaime flattened her hands on the table. "None of this is cool." The fear she had struggled to keep at bay started to claw its way out.

McKenna covered one of her hands with her own. "It's okay."

"How? How is this okay?" She started breathing faster. McKenna tightened her grip. "I'm happy to help Drew break his curse, but I'd like my daughter to be left out of this. Enough is enough. She's only ten!"

Ella's eyes widened, her whole face animated. "I can do this, Mom. I can help. I think that's why Jeremiah keeps hanging out. He knows I can help."

"But the shadow could come after you, and I don't know how to protect you from that."

"Mom, please. I can do this."

Jaime ran a hand through her hair again. "We'll have to discuss this." She pushed away from the table.

"We are discussing this." Ella jumped to her feet in seconds. "I want to do this."

"Let me talk to Drew."

"No. Drew isn't my dad. You don't have to talk to him at all."

"Ella." Jaime reached out to her daughter. Ella backed up to the door. With her lower lip trembling, she fled the room.

Jaime stood, ready to go after her. A hand on her back stopped her.

"Let me go. I'll make sure she doesn't run out of the office." McKenna smiled as she walked out the door.

Jaime sank back into her chair. "I'm not ready for any of this."

"None of us ever are," Tristan said.

Even though she didn't want to, Jaime gave her daughter some space. McKenna offered to look after her, so Jaime decided to deal with the other problem—Drew trying to fight the shadow by himself. When he let her into his small studio apartment, Jaime realized two things. One, she was setting foot in there for the first time. And two, Drew had an open bag on his bed with a few items of clothing stuffed into it.

Jaime crossed her arms. "Going somewhere?"

"Since this whole curse thing started because of me, I'm going to Frost Gap to end it on my own." Drew tossed a couple more shirts and pairs of pants into the bag.

"You mean, *we're* going to Frost Gap to end it, right?" Jaime voice was filled with ice. "Ella thinks she might have an idea of where the bow is buried."

He zipped the bag closed and faced her. He clutched the newly working disruptor in his hand. "No, I mean me. By myself."

Jaime raised an eyebrow. After the day she had had, she threatened to explode. She shook with the effort to control it. "The hell you are. You faced the shadow—no, his name was Richard Beauchamp—you faced him alone and nearly got yourself killed. Ella and I are coming with you."

"I can't let you do that."

It was the last straw. "You can't let me?" Jaime let all of her fury out. "Two nights ago, you told me you wanted Ella and me in your life. Completely, officially. And now, you're cutting us out?"

"No. I meant every word of that, but I don't want you to be a part of this. It's dangerous, Jaime." Drew's expression betrayed nothing.

"I know it's dangerous. That's why I can't let you go alone. Regardless of what you think needs to be done, your ancestors seem to think Ella and I are a part of this. We're coming." As much as she didn't want to put her daughter in harm's way, she couldn't argue with Ella's visions or her drawings. She was connected to this as much as Jaime.

Drew stuffed the disruptor into the pocket of his hoodie. "Jaime, I love you and Ella, and I don't want to put you in danger."

Jaime stood her ground. This issue meant too much to her not to back down. "We're already in danger. Melinda keeps telling me to keep you safe. And Ella can find the bow."

Drew's jaw twitched. "Just let me do this. Let me stop this."

"I want to go to Frost Gap with you and stop Beauchamp." She met his hazel-green eyes. "I don't want to lose you. I don't want to lose my daughter, either. We're in this together, Drew." She touched his cheek. "What do you want?"

His eyes darkened. "You. Safe."

Jaime scrunched her nose as she tossed her hands into the air. "We will be safe. We'll be safe together." Why couldn't she make him understand that the thought of losing him killed her inside? "Dammit, you're a part of me, a part of my life. I wake up thinking about you. I go to sleep thinking about you. I love you, Drew, and I want to keep you safe." She pulled one of his hands out of the hoodie and gripped it.

"Beauchamp wants to drive people apart. I think the key to stopping him is acting as a unit." She swallowed. "A family."

Drew softened. "If anything happened to you or Ella, I'd never forgive myself."

"I'd never forgive myself if anything ever happened to you." Jaime released him and stepped away. Her chest tightened as she studied him. "I have to pick up my daughter, who is also having a meltdown. Please don't do anything without us."

"I'll try."

Feeling a little better, Jaime left.

***

Guilt roared through Drew as he watched the woman he loved walk out. As soon as she closed the door behind her, he glanced at the unassuming box in the corner. He had sneaked the fiddle out of the office, grunting and fighting it the whole time. The box was filled with so much salt, it looked like he was planning to cook a lot of meat. The call to hold it thrummed in his head.

"I'm sorry, Jaime, but I have to stop this alone. For us."

23

Drew gritted his teeth as he fought the pull of the fiddle. The urge to touch it grew stronger with each passing minute. He knew he didn't have much time. Beauchamp's voice called out every once in a while, daring Drew to give in and quit. He fought against it so hard sweat dotted along his forehead and pooled in his palms.

He knew the shadow's name now, thanks to Jaime, and that information made the entity less frightening. Richard Beauchamp. Melinda's father. His ancestor, as well. How much anger had this man built up that he would try and kill his own flesh and blood? He *had killed* his own flesh and blood. His grandfather's brother. His uncle. But Drew intended to stop it once and for all. His disruptor rested at his side, and he refused to let Beauchamp knock it out of his hand this time.

All he had to do was find the last piece and make it there before the fiddle overwhelmed him.

He tore through the letters, scanning and searching for

any morsel, any hint of where he might find the waterfall or learn its name.

Jeremiah's love letters doted on Melinda, telling her he missed her and loved her. But none of them mentioned the waterfall.

Melinda's letters addressed to her son recounted stories about Jeremiah, his fiddle, and how he loved her. Every once in a while, she mentioned a darkness she felt around her son, a darkness that meant him harm.

Then he found the letter dated the day his great-grandfather was born, April 10, 1918.

My Dearest,

Don't go into the woods near the Smith's Plunge Waterfall alone. If even one drop of your blood touches the ground, he'll know, and he'll come for you. I pricked my finger with the sewing needle the other night, and he came up out of nowhere. Some salt around the house kept him away.

I thought I stopped him that night. But I've seen his shadow haunt this house and these woods. That's why I buried the bow. I thought he'd go away. But now I realize I was wrong. It's the fiddle he haunts.

But I swear I saw Jeremiah the other day. Bright and beautiful like I remember him. He seemed to keep the shadow away.

I gave the fiddle to a musician down in Boone. That seemed to make his shadow leave. Don't look for it, my boy. It's dangerous. Your grandfather is dangerous, even after death.

I think one prick of blood will set off the curse he set on this family. He swore on his dying breath he'd haunt my children forever until he eventually killed them all. I don't know if there's a way to stop him.

But, love, don't go in the woods and don't look for the fiddle. Stay away, whatever you do.

Love,

Your Mama

Drew set the letter down. He eyed the box in the corner, its siren song loud in his ears. "So, that's how you did it. Your hatred for Jeremiah held enough energy to curse us." He shivered. To know someone hated a person enough to try and kill their descendants after death terrified him. "I didn't even think such a thing was possible."

"You're mine," Beauchamp hissed as the box shook. "And you're all dead."

"This letter must have been what the legend grew out of," Drew mumbled. "But, Melinda, you didn't tell me how to break it."

Drew's heart sank. Even if he found the bow and put it with the fiddle, would that be enough? If he spilled his own blood, could that end it, too? Drew gripped the edge of the table as the fiddle called to him. What if Jaime was right? What if he did need her and Ella to break the curse? What if family was the key?

Old Mayor Beauchamp would resist, would go down with a fight. And that fight could get Jaime and Ella killed. He touched the disruptor lying next to him. Would it be enough to keep him safe?

But he learned the name of the waterfall, the most important part. Smith's Plunge. Ominous. He wondered who Smith had been and why he took a plunge, but he'd solve that mystery another time.

The box rattled louder. Wisps of dark smoke escaped from its wooden prison and disappeared into the air. Dark laughter followed as Beauchamp bulged out of the sides of the box.

No time left. Drew needed to make it to the waterfall in Frost Gap.

Even though night was falling, and he knew the timing

sucked, Drew packed up his car. He tossed his bag and a shovel into the backseat and the fiddle in the trunk. Its darkness nudged at him, threatening to break free at any moment. But the salt kept it at bay. He hoped it would hold long enough to get him there.

He thought about calling Jaime, asking her to come. Maybe he required her and Ella to end the curse. He rejected the idea as he slid into the driver's seat of his black Honda. It was his blood, his responsibility. He didn't want to drag a ten-year old out in the middle of the night.

So, he set out on his own. He gripped the steering wheel as he hit the highway. According to his map, the waterfall stood in a forest nestled somewhere at the bottom of Beech Mountain. People probably skied past it every winter. The trip lasted less than two hours. He cranked the metal, hoping it would drown out Beauchamp and the fiddle. He had to make it. He yearned to.

He worked to settle his nerves, preparing to make his stand and defeat Beauchamp once and for all. He knew the man was his great-great grandfather, but he didn't want to think of him as family. Especially since his shadow ghost wanted to kill him.

What made the man so spiteful and hateful? Was it because Jeremiah came from a lower class? Melinda and Jeremiah both seemed to think so, according to their letters. But still, to even try to hurt his own daughter and her children after his death appeared extreme.

Drew focused on the task at hand, breaking the curse. The one clue he found was Smith's Plunge Waterfall in the woods near Frost Gap, but he didn't think reaching it would be that easy.

The darkness stirred behind him, pushing against his mind. It felt like Beauchamp spoiled for a fight. The trunk muffled his groans, but they continued to ring in Drew's ears. He tightened his hold on the wheel, his knuckles white.

He exited off the highway and onto another quieter road. Fewer cars drove by, the lack of headlights enhancing the dark. Drew paid so much attention to his driving he almost missed the change in temperature. Even though the heat blasted, the interior started to freeze. Then his music, the headlights, and the engine cut in and out.

Drew swore as he pulled to the side of the road. Beauchamp had found a way through the salt. Black smoke pushed into the car. His prison no longer held him anymore. Drew wrapped his hand around the disruptor's handle. He sucked in his breath when the whole world went black.

Everything looked different. The dark forest enclosed the small cabin and its clearing, leaving only a tiny circle of light. Pieces of the porch lay broken on the ground. Someone or something cut the rocking chairs to bits. Indented marks from an ax covered the whole front of the cabin.

Jaime pushed through the forest, each heavy limb blocking her way. The path no longer existed. Underbrush and fallen branches covered it. She crawled under, stepped over, and shoved through until she reached the battered porch. Fear chilled her bones.

"Melinda?" Jaime set a foot on the first intact step. It creaked and bowed under her weight.

No one answered her call.

She gripped the remaining part of the banister and climbed to the next step. It broke the moment she stepped on it. Jaime held onto the banister as the stair crumbled beneath her feet. She jumped up the remainder of the stairs until she landed on the last bit of the porch. It also threatened to give way underneath her feet, but it stayed steady.

She called out again. "Melinda? Answer me. What happened?"

Still nothing.

Something was wrong. Something was terribly, horribly wrong. Jaime ran into the cabin. Light poured in through the windows and the open doorway. An empty wooden crib rocked in the corner. Tables and chairs lay on their sides, their legs broken. Pictures hung sideways on the wall, slash marks trailing through several of them. Jaime had never walked inside the cabin before, but she knew Melinda wouldn't leave it like that.

She saw movement out of the corner of her eye. Someone lay on the bed, and that person moved slowly. A groan filled the tiny space.

Jaime rushed over to find Melinda curled on the bed, fear in her green eyes.

"Melinda? Are you okay? What happened?" Jaime crouched next to her, her throat thick.

"He's found him. He's killing him." Melinda's eyes shone with tears.

"Who? Who is killing who?" Jaime laid a hand on Melinda's arm. "I don't understand."

Melinda flipped around and grabbed Jaime's wrist, her grip strong for a dead woman. Her nails dug into Jaime's skin. "My daddy. My daddy is killing Drew. You have to stop it. You have to help him."

"What?" So many questions ran through Jaime's mind. "That can't be. He's safe in his apartment. We're going to break the curse together."

"No." Melinda moved off the bed with unnatural speed. "He's gone to break it by himself. He can't do this alone." She grabbed Jaime's upper arms and shook her. "You have to be with him. You have to put the bow and the fiddle together. It's about an unbreakable bond."

The fear almost consumed her. "If that's true, I don't know where he is."

"Your little one does. She can track the fiddle. She can find the bow."

Jaime met the other woman's eyes and saw her own fear reflected there. "Ella is ten years old. I can't drag her into danger in the middle of the night."

"I know." Melinda softened. "But she's as much a part of this as you are. It's about family." Her face crumpled as she let go of Jaime. "This cabin, this world, is my prison, my punishment. I created that curse when I killed my daddy all those years ago. You have to stop it. I believe you, Drew, and Ella are the only ones who can." She placed a hand over her heart. "Please, wake up. Go find him. Wake up!"

"Mom! Mom! Wake up!" Ella's terrified voice penetrated through the fog of sleep, dragging Jaime out of the dream. Jaime blinked open her eyes to see her worried daughter standing next to the bed.

"Ella?" she mumbled. She saw the bright blue numbers on the alarm clock. They showed a couple of minutes past midnight. "What's wrong?"

"Drew's in trouble. We have to go now." She shook Jaime with all of her might. "We've got to get salt and the car. Come on! Come on!"

"What?" Still half-asleep, Jaime's brain moved in a sluggish rhythm. Drew in trouble? He couldn't be. The details of the dream came back to her piece by piece. The words Melinda said echoed what Ella told her. The meaning pushed through her sleepiness.

"Mom!" Ella pulled on her arm.

Jaime untangled herself from the sheets. "How do you know this?"

Before could answer, she saw Jeremiah's shimmering outline in her doorway. He stood tall, his hat on his head and his hands curled into fists. Determination filled his face.

"You warned her, like Melinda warned me." It wasn't a

question, but Jeremiah nodded in response. Melinda spoke the truth in the dream, and Drew was somewhere between Asheville and Frost Gap fighting off a shadow. Anger flared through the fear when she realized he had lied to her, but she knew she needed to rescue him.

She turned to her daughter. "Go get dressed and grab all the salt you can find, El. I'll be out there in a minute. Go! Go!"

Ella raced out of the room.

Jaime got dressed in record time and then sprinted down the hall into the living room. Ella waited for her, already dressed and brandished a box of salt. She lifted it for Jaime to see.

Jaime grabbed her keys. "You remember what the fiddle sounds like?"

"Yeah."

"Keep an ear out for it. But, El, promise me you'll stay in the car and out of the way." She held out her pinkie. "Promise?"

Ella hooked her pinkie around her mother's. "Promise." Clutching the box of salt, she raced for the car.

Jaime followed, hoping and praying they weren't too late.

24

The dark road loomed ahead of her. A few cars passed, but the road remained empty for the most part. Jaime struggled to keep the car steady at the speed limit. What if they were too late? What if the shadow killed Drew before they reached him? No, she refused to think about that. Melinda and Jeremiah wouldn't have warned her and Ella if it was too late. Jaime had to hold on to that belief. Every few minutes, she glanced at her daughter in the seat next to her.

"Anything yet?" she asked.

Ella sat still, her eyes closed. "No." She sounded frustrated. She wrinkled her brow, determination set on her young face.

"Keep trying. You can do this, baby." Jaime pushed away the negative thoughts telling her what a bad mother she was for dragging her daughter out in the middle of the night to face a dangerous shadow. Call her crazy, but she and Drew needed Ella to break this curse. She knew that in the bottom of her soul.

Jaime exited the interstate and headed up Highway 321.

The road became curvier and darker. The mountains didn't have that many street lights. Outside of the headlights, pitch black blanketed everything. Jaime cranked the heater in the car as high as it would go, but she continued to shiver, chilled to the bone.

Ella's eyes popped open. "It's here." The color drained from her cheeks. "The shadow is there, too."

"Where?" Jaime couldn't see a thing.

"On the side of the road, right up ahead." Ella pointed to the left.

Jaime slowed down and concentrated on everything the headlights touched. She gasped when she saw Drew's car still on the side of the road. She pulled in behind it and cut the engine. Snatching a flashlight and a box of salt from the bag in the back seat, she pinned Ella with a look. "Bundle up and don't move."

Jaime moved like lightning, not stopping to think it through. She jumped out of the car, clicked on the flashlight, and ran. Drew's Civic was quiet and dark. She lifted the cold car door handle. Gathering her courage, she trained the small circle of light on it and swung it open.

She had witnessed Drew engulfed in the shadow before, but she never saw the shadow take over an entire space. Inky blackness filled every nook and cranny. She pointed the light on the dark, but it swallowed the light whole. Her flashlight blinked in and out. The cold and the dark seemed to grow worse.

She had no time to waste.

Jaime opened the salt and grabbed a handful. She tossed it into the air. The shadow parted where the particles touched. For a moment, she saw Drew lying across the seat. His chest lifted up and down in small, light movements.

She dove through the opening as the darkness started to close around her. The iciness stole her breath. Even as she wrapped her coat tighter around herself, the cold seeped in. Little ice crystals formed on her skin in the places where the shadow touched.

"You're too late," Beauchamp hissed in her ear.

"I'm not. I can't be." She fought her way to Drew's side. She tossed more salt into the air, listening for the satisfying howl of pain from Richard Beauchamp, the man who wanted to destroy his own great-great grandson. She needed to remember the shadow had a name. Names held power.

She gritted her teeth as she crawled to Drew. "I know who you are," she said to the shadow. "You were once the mayor of a small town called Frost Gap. You had two daughters, Melinda and Esther. You must have loved them."

A hiss surrounded her. "Nothing matters but revenge. Melinda betrayed me. Chose that boy over her own family, over her future. I won't rest until I've erased every last trace of him from this earth." The dark smoke closed in again, taking away the light.

"Mom!" Ella called from behind.

"Stay back, El. Don't move." She tossed more salt into the air. How much salt was in the box anyway? Would it be enough to keep the thing that used to be Beauchamp away from them? Jaime didn't have time to dwell. Her flashlight still worked against all the odds. In the momentary light, she found Drew's wrist and touched it. He still had a pulse. She breathed a sigh of relief.

"Drew." She shook him. "Drew, you have to wake up. We have to get the fiddle to the waterfall. We can't do this without you."

At her touch, Drew stirred. His eyes fluttered open. "Jaime?" His voice cracked.

"Yeah."

Beauchamp cut her celebration short. He regrouped and

closed in on them once again, stealing the warmth and the air.

"You can die with him for all I care. And I'll take that brat of yours, too." Nothing human remained inside Beauchamp. Nothing hovered in that dark smoke but hate, anger, and misery. To prove his point, a small tunnel formed past Jaime and out of the car.

A tendril of smoke wrapped around Ella's arm. She screamed.

"No!" Jaime tried to run through the tunnel, but it collapsed around her. "Ella!"

Light burst in front of her daughter, pushing the dark back and away from Ella. Jeremiah stood between Beauchamp and his prey. His whole body burned brighter than she'd ever seen it.

"Go! Find the treasure. Break the curse. I can't hold him for long." Jeremiah's sad eyes met Jaime's. "It's time for this to end."

Ella ran to her mother. Jaime stepped out of the car and hugged her tight. She then pushed Ella toward their car. "Get in." She helped Drew to his feet. He leaned heavily on her. Jeremiah's light waned. The darkness pieced together and crept in again.

"Drew, are you okay? Can you drive? If I take the fiddle, can you drive?" Why didn't she think to call the rest of the team for backup? In her hurry, she'd forgotten.

"I don't know." Drew doubled over, sucking in air. "Maybe?"

Two circles of light pulled up behind Jaime's car. They cut out as a van door slid open.

"Oh, my God." A flashlight bobbed in their direction.

She thought she recognized the voice, but she prepared to meet a stranger. She scrambled for a plausible explanation. When the owner of the flashlight came closer, Jaime realized she didn't have to. McKenna held it as she ran. Aaron, Tabitha, and Tristan followed in her wake.

"How?" Jaime stuttered the word, trying to understand.

"Ella is a fast texter and pretty good at directions," McKenna explained.

Jaime sagged with relief. She was proud her daughter had stayed one step ahead of her.

"That ghost is a beautiful sight," Aaron murmured.

"We have to hurry," McKenna sighed. "He's weakening."

Tristan and Aaron jumped in and helped Drew into the passenger side of his car. Tristan jingled the keys. "Where are we going?"

Jaime wrapped her arms around herself. "Frost Gap."

"Floorboard!" Drew yelled.

"What?" Aaron asked.

"The disruptor. On the floorboard. Take it." He then passed out in the seat.

Aaron grabbed the weapon and climbed into the backseat.

When Tristan popped the trunk, Jaime sprang into action. She grabbed the box with the fiddle and moved it to her own car. She poured a hefty amount of salt on it before slamming the trunk shut. Beauchamp howled and dispersed into the air. Jeremiah faded away before Jaime could thank him. Was there anything of his energy left to thank?

At last, she threw herself into the driver's seat of her own car and cranked the engine. She hoped they could find the waterfall in the dark because the salt might not hold Beauchamp. She feared he'd crawl out and attack Ella again.

She drove in silence, leading the caravan. She hurried down the winding roads, easing along the curves. At least no one else traveled the road this late at night, and the moon beamed full and bright above them. After several minutes, she heard Beauchamp rumbling in the trunk. Her headlights flickered. He was gaining strength.

Beside her, Ella's face paled. She closed her eyes again, her brow furrowed.

Jaime touched her shoulder. "We're almost there. We can do this."

With the GPS guiding her, she found the road and made the left turn. Halfway down it, the pavement changed to gravel. Civilization gave way to dark, dark woods. She swallowed. She had never ventured this far away from a city or a town before. And in the mountains, long stretches of nothing spread out in all directions. The absence of light or sound freaked her out a little.

"This is it!" Ella exclaimed, her eyes snapping open. "The bow is here. I can hear it."

"Ella, baby. This is going to sound like a weird question, but can you find a waterfall?" Jaime kept her eyes on the dirt road, not daring to look away for a second.

"I'll try."

"Good girl. You try as hard as you can while I try to find out where we are."

A roar echoed from the trunk, and loud banging followed. Beauchamp had worked his way out of his salty prison. With no disruptor and half a box of salt, Jaime began to shake. She didn't know what to do. She and Drew planned to do this in the daylight, not pitch-black darkness. Thank goodness Drew rode in two cars back.

Out of the corner of her eye, Jaime saw a soft glow. She slowed the car down. The glow hovered in the middle of four huge trees and formed into the shape of a woman. The legend she discovered flooded back to her. The lady haunting the Frost Gap woods, searching for someone.

"Melinda." Jaime breathed. She pulled the car over and parked. She gripped her daughter's hand. "Stay close to me.

Whatever happens." She popped on the flashlight and jumped out of the car. Tendrils of smoke spewed out of the trunk.

Ella hopped out next to her. "I know which way to go." Her eyes shone in the low light.

Drew struggled to get out of the car, his whole body heavy. When Beauchamp attacked him, he had battled as long as he could, but his strength gave out. He almost made it to the woods, ready to break the curse on his own. Beauchamp's shadow overtook him before he reached them. He grabbed onto Jaime's voice when she broke through, an anchor in his black storm keeping him grounded. Her voice had called him home and gave him the will to fight back.

Filled with renewed determination, Drew prepared to get rid of Beauchamp for good.

As he stumbled to the trunk, Aaron pressed the disruptor into Drew's chest. "You'll need this. Don't drop it this time."

Drew's fingers closed around it. "I won't." He patted both Tristan and Aaron on the backs with his free hand. Knowing his friends waged war alongside him gave him even more resolve. "Let's get the girls and do this." He raised his head and saw a woman's glowing form in the woods. Melinda. His great-great grandmother.

"She's beautiful, like she was in my vision," Tristan inched away from the car, his eyes wide.

Drew grabbed the shovel, and Jaime approached with the fiddle. Ella, McKenna, and Tabitha ran behind her. Wisps of darkness escaped from the box. Drew clutched the disruptor tightly.

He nodded to Ella. "Lead the way."

They trudged through the woods, flashlights and the full

moon lighting the way. Jaime held Ella's hand, and Drew held onto Jaime's elbow. Everyone else followed behind.

Pressure built in Drew's chest. Beauchamp was pushing through his salty prison, chomping at the bit.

"Give up," he seethed. "Give up like all the others."

"No!" Drew knew he wasn't the only Keane to activate and to try to stop the curse. In his research he learned about his uncle who had died too soon—the older brother his dad loved very much. Drew chose not to let that happen to him, and unlike his uncle, Jaime, Ella, and his team stood with him.

The sound of rushing water hit his ears, pulling him out of his own head. The waterfall! He exchanged a look with Jaime. They were so close.

"Right up here," Ella announced. They followed her up a hill and stopped when they reached the top. The small water-fall, the one where Melinda and Jeremiah met and fell in love, rushed down the cliff below them.

"Where's the spot?" Drew asked.

Ella stood among the four huge trees and stamped her feet. "Right here."

Drew set his stuff down and picked up the shovel. Aaron and Tristan joined him with two more shovels. With everyone else holding lights over the spot, they drove their shovels into the cold, hard ground. Drew's muscles bunched as he lifted the dirt away. He strained with each load. After a while, the shovels hit something solid.

Jaime and Ella dropped to their knees and dug with Drew until they unearthed a box, the wooden box Ella had drawn a week earlier. Drew and Jaime worked together to lift it out of the dirt, setting it on top of the ground. As the first light of morning appeared, Drew opened it.

A bow lay inside. It was a little dirty, and a few bugs had decided to make the box their home. But, otherwise, it remained intact. Drew held his breath, Beauchamp's shadow pressing against him.

"Don't do it, boy," Beauchamp hissed. Darkness oozed out of the fiddle and took the form of Beauchamp himself. He stood, a proud, broad-shouldered man with glowing, red eyes. He whipped out his arms and snatched Ella off her feet. His shadow coiled around her like a snake. "I'll destroy everything you love."

"No!" Jaime tossed all the contents of the salt box at Beauchamp. Nothing happened. He shook off the salt, his shadow choking off Ella's air.

"Surrender, boy, and the child lives." Beauchamp sneered.

***

Fear crawled up Jaime's spine. Beauchamp was going to destroy someone she loved. It didn't matter to him whether that person was Ella or Drew. Drew shoved the hard, sleek disruptor into her hand. She turned it on and pointed it at Beauchamp. Then she pulled the trigger. Beauchamp broke apart, but immediately reformed next to Ella before she could move.

Jaime raised the disruptor again.

"I can do this all night," Beauchamp said.

She drew her shoulders back. "Me, too."

He dove for her. She burst him apart again.

"Take me instead." The disruptor never wavered.

Beauchamp chuckled. "Oh, I'll take you alright. You're going to die along with him. Just wait your turn."

"No. This ends now." Drew swiped a hand through the air, his jaw set. Beauchamp whirled to face him. Drew raised his hands in surrender. "I'm all yours."

Beauchamp released Ella and flew at Drew, engulfing him in seconds.

Jaime was losing him, second by second, and in that instant, she knew she couldn't. She loved him. She admitted it to herself: she loved him. Her life felt empty without him in it. She thrust her chin upward and squared her shoulders.

Melinda appeared out of thin air and wrapped her arms protectively around Ella. She met Jaime's eyes. "Go."

Jaime clutched the disruptor. She jumped into the inky blackness. It broke apart as she marched through, every shot breaking down Beauchamp's energy. She clutched Drew's hand and pulled him out. When they cleared the smoke, she picked up the bow and placed it on the fiddle.

Nothing happened.

Beauchamp's shadow pieced itself back together. He roared, and the air around them picked up speed. Leaves joined the whirlwind, whipping the cold air around them. Jaime and Drew stood inside it.

"You should've let me go," Drew yelled over the roar. "Ella is more important."

"She is, but you're important, too. I love you, Drew!" She placed a hand on the fiddle and the bow and grabbed Drew's shirt with the other. She pressed her mouth against his in a deep kiss.

His hand covered hers.

Jaime swore she felt the earth shift.

Then another hand joined theirs. Jaime eased back to see Ella kneeling with them. She and Drew embraced her. The three of them huddled against the storm.

Light burst from the fiddle, arcing upward through their joined hands. It tingled with heat and joy. It pushed through the tornado, spearing out in all directions. The light surrounded Beauchamp and killed every part of his shadow. He screamed as he blew apart, leaving nothing behind.

Jaime turned off the disruptor, and the fiddle's light grew brighter.

It swirled and twirled before forming the shape of a door. Jeremiah stepped through, holding out a hand to Melinda. "My treasure." He appeared like he had in Jaime's dream, full of color and life. He snatched his hat off his head and cradled it to his chest.

Ella stood with her mouth hanging open, watching as Melinda took his hand. Melinda nodded to the three of them. Together, the couple walked through the door. As soon as they vanished inside, the door burst into tiny lights and dissipated.

Ella moved her hand away. Jaime and Drew lifted theirs off the fiddle and bow. Jaime checked her hand and detected no sign that the light had come through it.

She tugged her daughter into her arms once more and squeezed. "Are you okay?"

"Yeah, Mom." Ella hugged her back.

Two strong arms hugged them both. "Thank you. For everything," Drew said.

They let go, and Jaime turned to see the fiddle and the bow still there, lying together in the leaves. Nothing sinister rose from them.

"Well, that was one hell of a ride." Aaron jogged to them, the rest of the team on his heels. The wind tossed his short, brown hair in every direction. He slapped Drew on the back. "But I don't want to do it again."

25

For the first time in a long time, Drew had wrestled with a ghost, and he won. He lay on the cold, hard ground and watched the morning light appear through the trees. The fiddle stayed quiet, nothing pulling at him and begging him to touch it. The shadow didn't try to steal his air. He was free. Completely and totally free.

"How are you doing?" Tristan kicked his foot.

"Better, man." Drew rested his hands on his stomach. "A hundred times better."

His best friend sat down next to him. "Why didn't you tell me? Why didn't you tell any of us?"

Drew sighed and draped an arm across his forehead. He reached for the bill of his cap, but his hand met air. He sighed. It probably fell off somewhere in his car. He hoped he hadn't lost it.

He groaned and sat up. "I wanted to protect everybody. This curse belonged to me." He rested his arm on his raised knee. "It was something I had to do."

"Right." Tristan narrowed his green eyes. "And when I went after Dr. Smith on my own to protect everyone?"

Drew shook his head. "I was ready to kick your ass."

"Well." Tristan smacked him on the back a little too hard. Drew winced. "Same goes for me." He leaned back on his hands and peered at the sky. "You should've told me, man. I don't like the idea of losing another friend to a ghost."

"Yeah, I know. I don't, either."

They sat in silence for a little while as everyone else checked on each other.

Jaime stepped in front of Drew, blocking the light.

Tristan shook Drew's shoulder. "This is my cue to leave." He stood and headed away from them, swishing through the underbrush.

Jaime held out a hand. Drew took it and climbed to his feet.

"Jaime, I..." He didn't get the rest of the words out.

She grabbed the front of his shirt, jerked him towards her, and kissed him. She then pushed him away. "Don't you ever sneak off and scare me like that again. Ever."

Drew rubbed the back of his neck. "You're right. I'm sorry. You should've been there from the start. You and Ella." His fingers trailed down the fabric of her jacket. "How is Ella?"

"She's going to be okay. She's sleeping in the Restless Spirits' van right now." Jaime wrapped her arms around herself. "I can't believe we did that. We actually broke a real live curse together." She met his eyes. "Never in my wildest dreams did I ever think that was possible."

"Me neither. But we did it." And everyone came out alive and safe. Drew enveloped her in his arms and buried his face in her hair. Her soft, perfect, flower-scented hair. For a moment, he thought the shadow would kill her and Ella, but that hadn't happened. They all made it through the dark night, along with the rest of his team. He thought of different ways to thank them. Maybe bake them a cake or wash the van for the next few months. Aaron was never going to let him forget this.

"What are you thinking?" Jaime asked.

"About how I never want to let you or Ella go." He raised his head and tucked a strand of dark hair behind Jaime's ear. "You're both part of my world now." He chuckled. "You're stuck with me."

She laughed along with him. "There's no one else I'd rather be stuck with." She sighed. "But I need to get some sleep."

"I know a perfect place, not far from here."

———

Drew's childhood home, or the apartment he called his childhood home, charmed Jaime. She hadn't expect a small three-bedroom apartment nestled back in the woods on the side of the mountain. When Jaime walked into the living room and opened the big picture window, her breath caught in her throat. Boone spread out below her, and the mountains framed the small town.

"Wow!" Ella walked up beside her. "This is amazing. Why don't we have a view like this?"

"Because we had limited options." Jaime turned to Drew, who closed the front door. "This is gorgeous."

"My mom got lucky. She was friends with the realtor and was able to get this place for a steal." He joined them at the window. "Mrs. Barnes, the realtor, wanted to help my mom get away from my dad."

"I'm sorry."

"It's okay. I got to see this view every day."

Ella pressed her hands against the glass. "It's like we're on top of the world."

"Exactly," Drew agreed.

"Can I see this view from my room?" Ella beamed at Drew.

"Your room? Already claiming this apartment, huh? And I thought you didn't like me." He nodded to the hallway behind them. "You're in the first bedroom on the right. That was my sister's room, and yeah, you've got the view."

Without saying another word, she dashed off to have a look.

"Are you sure your mom doesn't mind us staying here?" Jaime stepped away from the window.

"Not at all. It's my home, too."

"I know." Jaime shrugged. After she moved out, she had gotten used to calling her parents first and asking if she could visit. Even though her mom usually knew she was coming ahead of time, they always insisted that she call. The idea of walking into her childhood home unannounced felt strange, and especially when she brought Ella. Her parents preferred that everything be perfect before they arrived.

She wandered around the room, taking in the overstuffed sectional couch and chairs. A widescreen TV covered almost one whole wall. "So, which bedroom do I get to claim?"

"Mom's. It's all the way in the back."

"Good. Because I need a nap." She called the college earlier to tell them she needed the day off, and she would deal with Ella's school the next day. With a smile, she walked to the bedroom, dropped onto the soft bedspread, and fell fast asleep. She didn't dream of anything.

A few hours later, Ella sat by the big picture window and studied the mountains spread out before her. She loved the view so much she wanted to stay there forever. As much as she loved the sights, though, the music sounded better. Every object in the house hummed in perfect harmony. Even the fiddle and the bow were in harmony, still in the trunk of the car. Neither one held a menacing note or screeched out of tune anymore. They really did need to be together.

Ella still felt the chill of the shadow, but she also remembered Melinda's calming presence. As far as she knew, ghosts made places cold, not warm. She remembered how icy her bedroom felt. But Melinda made her feel warm and safe. That memory pushed away the one with the shadow.

Ella thought about the whole ghost hunting thing. It had been scary, but kind of cool at the same time. Maybe she'd hunt ghosts when she grew up. She thought about asking Aaron for a job someday.

"The view is amazing, isn't it?" Drew pulled up a chair and joined her at the window.

"Yeah, it's nice." He still invaded her space, but not as much anymore. Over the last couple of weeks, he came when she and her mom needed him, even if he did try to break the curse without them. But he didn't seem too bad. She refused to hope, but maybe he'd stick around for a while.

"Still hate me?" he asked.

Ella cocked her head to side, thinking. "Maybe not as much."

Drew nodded. "I'll take that as a ringing endorsement." He reached out and ruffled her hair. "You're not so bad yourself."

Ella tried not to smile, but she couldn't help it.

"I knew you could do it." He looked at the view. After a few moments, he said, "I know what it's like not to have a dad around."

"Doesn't make any difference to me." Ella shrugged. *What a lie!* It made a huge difference. She always felt a stab of jealousy when she watched Kelly with her dad. She wondered what that would be like, having a dad of her own.

"I get it. My dad spent most of his time drinking and not being there." He took a breath and faced her. "Ella, I'm not trying to be your dad, but I'd like to be your friend."

Ella curled her arms around her knees. "But what if you don't stick around?" Her stomach twisted. She'd revealed her biggest fear to Drew. She waited for him to call her a baby.

"Fair question." Drew nodded. "I don't know what's going to happen between your mom and me, but I will always be your friend. Whatever you need, whenever you need me, I'll be there." He held out his fist. "I can promise you that."

She pressed her lips together. None of the other guys had ever said that to her, but she thought Drew sounded sincere, kind of like when an object sang a sweet tune. She bumped his fist. "Cool."

Together, they turned back to the window and watched the clouds roll by.

Two Weeks Later

Stop fussing with the fiddle and come to dinner." Jaime swatted Drew on the arm.

"It was crooked." He stepped back and studied his handiwork. He and Jaime decided to hang the fiddle and the bow on the wall of his office at Restless Spirits. He figured if the curse ever came back, Restless Spirits seemed the safest place for it to be. Plus, Jaime said that it didn't go with the decor in her living room anymore. He thought it probably just gave her the creeps.

He adjusted his Duke cap, which he had found two weeks earlier on the floorboard of his car, and stepped out of the office to see the spread of food covering the conference table. Turkey, dressing, ham, and more sides than he thought possible.

Before everyone went off to their respective Thanksgivings, Aaron had suggested a pre-Thanksgiving meal for them. Everybody agreed.

McKenna tried to keep Tristan out of the pumpkin pie, Jaime helped Ella fill up her plate, and Tabitha told Aaron he didn't need to take half the turkey.

"You know, I bought this turkey." Aaron measured a huge chunk and positioned the large knife at the end. "I can eat all of it if I want."

"Share." Tabitha rolled her eyes.

"You better get in here before Aaron eats everything." Tristan sat down with a slice of his hard-won pie.

"You haven't even had dinner yet," McKenna argued as she and her full plate settled next to him.

"Someone has to sample the pie." He placed a noisy kiss on her cheek.

"We saved you a seat over here." Jaime smiled as she patted the chair next to her.

Drew slid into it and removed his cap. He plopped it onto Ella's head, making her laugh. It sank down past her ears and covered her eyes. During the last two weeks, he and Ella had formed a tight friendship. Since he could leave the office earlier, he picked her up from school. They spent the afternoon driving around and guessing which ghosts haunted which buildings. As a bonus, he heard all the juicy fifth-grade gossip before her mother did.

He picked up his plate, ready to fill it to the brim with all the food.

Jaime touched his chin and turned him to face her. "I love you." She kissed him, sending tingles through his whole body.

Family. That's how Drew saw them. None of them were related by blood, but they loved each other. And that's all he ever wanted. Well, that, and for the ghosts to stop beating up on him.

He lifted his glass. "To the ghosts."

"To the ghosts!" Everyone echoed.

And thank goodness, there wasn't a ghost in sight that wanted to kill him.

I'm grateful and humble that I got to tell Drew's story. I'd hoped the first book would get published; the second was icing on the cake.

I delved into my own family history for this adventure. Drew's ghost is loosely based off a story my Nanny told her younger sister a long time ago. My Aunt Maxine shared this story along with many others about Nanny with me in two separate letters when I was sixteen. I cherish those letters, and I'm grateful for them. I think Nanny would enjoy this series.

While Asheville and Boone are real places, everywhere else is fictional. Sadly, you won't actually find Restless Spirits, Inc. on Haywood Street in Asheville. Nor is there a Frost Gap.

Thank you to John Hartness, Melissa Gilbert, and everyone at Falstaff Books for taking a chance on this series. I'm having way too much fun writing it.

My thanks to Susan Roddey, one of my best friends, for editing this book and making sure it looks its best.

I'm not tech smart nor do I know anything about building

stuff. Or science in general. The Ghost Disruptor and I owe a big thank you to Joy Jones and Gabriel Mills. They gave me excellent suggestions and tips. Any science and tech mistakes are my own.

Thank you to Gail Martin and Lucy Blue for taking a novice author under your wings.

To Jaime Wurth. I hope you don't mind having a character named after you.

Alexandra Christian, Tally Johnson, and Susan and Bill Roddey, you're the best friends a girl ever had. We've got to get together again at some point!

Jonathan, Lanette, Mom, Dad, and all the nieces and nephews, you're the best.

To Michael. Thank you for being the best husband ever.

Thank you to all the readers who bought and read *White Spirit*. This book wouldn't be here without you. I hope you enjoy Drew's story as much as you did Tristan's.

ABOUT THE AUTHOR

Amy Ravenel has done a bit of everything – waitressing, customer service, teaching, librarianship. But writing has been the only thing she's ever wanted to do. She has a deep love for bookstores, the mountains, and all sorts of geeky things. A native North Carolinian, she grew up in the foothills near the inspiration for Mayberry. Today, she lives with her epically-bearded husband and her epically-furry cats.

www.ingramcontent.com/pod-product-compliance
Lightning Source LLC
Chambersburg PA
CBHW050251110726
47898CB00007B/2372